The Giants of the Baroka Valley

The Guardians of Elestra #2

Thom Jones

Peekaboo Pepper Books

This book is dedicated to my kids Galen and Aidan (the focus group readers/editors and the source of so many of my ideas), and Dinara (whose editing consists of scribbling with markers all over the pages I print), and my wife Linda who is like a swash-buckling pirate with her editor's pencil.

The Giants of the Baroka Valley, Guardians of Elestra #2

Also available in the Guardians of Elestra series:

#1   The Dark City
#3   The Desert of the Crescent Dunes
#4   The Seven Pillars of Tarook
#5   The Eye of the Red Dragon
#6   The Misty Peaks of Dentarus (Summer 2011)

To learn more about Elestra, including maps, history, Tobungus' blog, Glabber's menu, and contests that allow readers to submit ideas for new characters, places, or other magical things, please visit:

www.guardiansofelestra.com

CONTENTS

1 Were We Dreaming?

Derek Hughes yawned and stretched in his bed. He had just had the most amazing dream. He closed his eyes to remember the details. In the dream, he and his twin sister Deanna had traveled to a magical land called Elestra where they battled an evil wizard named Eldrack. Their grandfather was captured by Eldrack, but he managed to tell them that they were members of a magical family of Mystical Guardians who protected Elestra. They had recovered the first of fifteen moonstones and were preparing to go off in search of the second. They had spent the previous day at a huge library reading about Elestra and its fifteen moons which acted as gateways to other worlds.

He looked over at the other bed and saw Deanna just starting to stir from a deep sleep. He couldn't wait for her to wake up. He wanted to tell her everything about his dream. "Deanna," he said. "Wake up. I've got to tell you about the most incredible dream."

"Huh?" Deanna mumbled. "Mmmmm," was all she could say.

Derek decided to open the curtains and let the sun wake her up. He walked over to the window and threw the curtains aside. He looked out and froze.

"I'm up, I'm up," Deanna sputtered as the sunlight shot into her eyes. She rubbed her blue eyes and looked at Derek. "What's wrong?" she asked.

"I wanted to tell you about a dream I had," Derek began. "It was the most unbelievable thing ever." He stopped for a few seconds.

"I had a great dream too," Deanna added, as she reached onto her nightstand and grabbed her silver braided headband and put it into her long brown hair. Her grandfather had given her the headband, which was decorated with silver moon-shaped beads, for her eleventh birthday. "We went to this really weird place called Elestra and met the oddest mushroom man." She could see that he was barely listening to her. "Derek!" she blurted out.

"Yeah, yeah, Tobungus, the mushroom man," he mumbled. He turned to her, and she saw that his face was white. "I don't think we were dreaming."

"What?" Deanna whispered. She struggled from under her blankets, jumped out of bed, and ran to the window.

Outside, she saw a bustling crowd moving about the once dusty streets of Amemnop. "Then we really are in Elestra," she murmured.

Memories of the past two days flooded back into her mind. They had started the Fountain of the Six Kingdoms two days earlier and lifted the Spell of Darkness that Eldrack had cast upon the city. Now, Amemnop was becoming the City of Light again, as it was known in its earlier days. It had always been the capital of Magia, the magical kingdom in Elestra, but now people began to enjoy their lives again.

She recalled meeting Iszarre, the Great Wizard who worked as a cook at Glabber's Grub Hut. After they found the first moonstone, he told them that he had to visit King Barado to update him on their progress. Before he left, he had told them to look up the Baroka Valley to learn more about their next adventure.

Deanna turned from the window, pulled a purple shirt and jeans from the closet, and quickly got dressed. She loaded up her backpack and made sure to include an extra change of clothes.

Before Derek put his clothes in his backpack, she asked, "Do you want me to change the color of your shirt? Iszarre told me we could do that, and I found the spell in the Book of Spells." The Book of Spells was contained inside a small book-shaped locket. Their grandfather had given them the locket and the powerful Wand of Ondarell in the Cave of Imprisonment. When the locket was opened, the large, tattered Book of Spells appeared.

"No," Derek began, "I'll just keep the shirt green for now."

Derek wrapped his rope wristband with moon-shaped granite stones around his left wrist and ran a comb through his blond hair. "Don't you think it's time for a haircut?" Deanna teased.

"What? It's not even to my shoulders yet," Derek answered. He checked to make sure that they had everything that they would need for the day. They went downstairs into the diner and had huge stacks of pancakes and strawberries.

They were nearly finished eating when they heard a strange 'clop, clop, clop' sound. When they turned, they saw their friend Tobungus, the mushroom man, walking toward them in a pair of Dutch wooden shoes.

Tobungus was a little over four feet tall,

with stubby arms poking out of his mushroom stem body. He had a collection of outlandish shoes to match his bizarre behavior.

"Tobungus," Derek said, "why in the world are you wearing those ridiculous shoes?"

"You have no sense of style, Goober," Tobungus answered. "These shoes may not be comfortable, but they make a great noise when I walk on the wooden sidewalks outside. It's like they're yelling to all of Amemnop that Tobungus is coming."

"My name is Derek! Is that really so hard?" Tobungus was always forgetting their names. This was a common trait for mushroom people, but the names that Tobungus chose to call them were usually ridiculous.

Tobungus waved off Derek's remark and looked at their plates. "Panpies. I love panpies."

"Pancakes," Deanna corrected. "When have you had pancakes?"

"Glabber makes all sorts of stuff from your world. He thinks it makes him exotic." Glabber was the snake wizard who worked with Iszarre in the diner and helped to guard against Eldrack's plans to conquer Elestra.

"Well, we can't sit and talk about food all day," said Deanna, anxious for their next adventure to begin. "We have to get back to the library."

Tobungus closed his shoe bag and said, "Yes, yes. Yesterday you said that we might be going to the Baroka Valley. I'll head over to the Goose Lot and arrange for transport."

"The Goose Lot?" Derek repeated.

"Sure, geese are the fastest way to get most places in Elestra. You can meet me there when you're done." Tobungus stood up and clopped his way back into the street.

"Do you suppose he's the weirdest creature in the universe?" Deanna asked.

"No," Derek answered. "I have a feeling that we'll find much weirder creatures here in Elestra."

They left the diner and headed across town to the State Library of Magia where they would ask the magical books questions about the Baroka Valley. After a few minutes of walking, they noticed that many people seemed to be watching them. They were beginning to feel uneasy and picked up their pace toward the library.

Deanna was just about to pull out the Wand of Ondarell when an old woman squawked, "Look there. The tall boy with the blond hair and the girl with the long brown hair. They're the new Mystical Guardians who started the Fountain."

The other people on the street waved, and a few came up to thank them. They suddenly felt very safe in Amemnop, and they wondered if they really needed to leave the city before Iszarre returned from his meeting with King Barado.

"If this is a dream, it's not that bad," Derek whispered to Deanna.

"Come on," she said, pulling him away from the growing crowd. They walked for another ten minutes before they came to the fifteen foot doors that led to the most unusual library they had ever visited.

2 The Bad Book Fairy

Just as she had done on their first visit to the State Library of Magia, Deanna stood gaping at the towering walls of books. The candles spiraling up the walls seemed to highlight that the library reached into the sky. Derek pulled her along to the main desk where they would search for information about their next adventure.

A tiny librarian, no taller than six inches, wearing a flowing dress at least eight inches long, smiled at them from behind silver-rimmed glasses. "Can I help you?" she asked politely.

"I hope so," Deanna replied. "We're looking for information about the Baroka Valley. We don't know anything about it, so anything you have will be great."

Looking at the book-lined walls, the little woman called out, "Show me books about the Baroka Valley." A shower of sparks zipped around the room and settled on at least fifty books. She looked surprised at the number of sparkling books. "Book fairies," she finally called, "bring half of the books to table four."

A swarm of book fairies shot up from under the desk and swooped around the shelves. The book fairies were tiny flying creatures that used their magic to collect books from the high shelves for the library's visitors. The fairies' silvery wings shimmered in the candle light and made their pale green skin look like it had its own inner light.

The fairies flew down from the shelves towing books with magical golden threads. In less than a minute, a stack of nearly thirty books stood on the table where Derek and Deanna were setting their backpacks.

Deanna reached for the nearest book and pulled it in front of her. She touched the Wand of Ondarell to the book's cover and said, "*Explanatum.*" She felt a rush of magic flow through her as the book shuddered. "Tell me about the Baroka Valley," she said to the book.

The book opened to page 1, and a deep voice said:

The Baroka Valley lies on the western fringes of Magia, past the Bagayama Mountains, before the Crystal Divide. The eastern border of the Baroka Valley is the River of the Dragon's Breath.

"Can you give us any details about the Baroka Valley?" Deanna asked. "What's it like?

The book shuddered, flipped itself open to page 4, and said:

> Many people in Magia call the
> Baroka Valley the Big Valley
> because everything in the valley is
> so large. Birds lay eggs that can
> feed an entire village, grains of sand
> are the size of boulders, trees reach
> up through the clouds, and fleas are
> larger than normal dogs.

"What is the easiest way to reach the Baroka Valley?" Deanna asked.

The book sounded as if it was clearing its throat and continued:

> Visitors can only reach the Baroka
> Valley from the air because of the
> River of the Dragon's Breath.

"What's the River of the Dragon's Breath?" Derek asked excitedly.

The same deep voice returned:

The River of the Dragon's Breath is a river that flows over an underground lava chamber which sits under Cauldron Mountain, the most active volcano in Magia. The heat from the lava boils the river's waters and causes geysers to shoot up from the river's surface. All of the sadness in the Kingdom collects in the river and boils off with the steam. At the bottom of Cauldron Mountain, the river cools and becomes the River of Tranquility which flows into Amemnop.

"Thank you," Deanna said. The book closed and hopped back onto the stack. The next eight books told them the same information about the Baroka Valley. "What should we ask next?" she asked Derek.

"Well, we need to figure out where to look for the moonstone, so maybe something about magical locations," he answered.

She turned to the tenth book and said, "Tell me about magical locations in the Baroka Valley."

A soft voice replied:

There are forty-six highly magical locations in the Baroka Valley, according to the latest Survey of Magical Activity in Magia. Do you have a specific magical location in mind?

"I'm not sure which location we want," Deanna said. She thought about the types of places that they might be looking for. "Are there any stories about a moonstone being hidden in the Baroka Valley or about Baladorn visiting the area?"

The voice returned, *"There is no reference to a moonstone or Baladorn within this book."*

Deanna thought of other questions, but nothing seemed right. Derek wondered if they were asking about the wrong Mystical Guardian. He realized that since Mindoro was Baladorn's son, he would have been responsible for hiding the second moonstone in the Baroka Valley. They had seen Mindoro frozen in a fog-filled glass tube when they explored the Cave of Imprisonment, where thirteen generations of wizards from their family, including their grandfather, were being held captive by Eldrack.

Derek picked up the wand and said to the eleventh book, "Are there any stories about Mindoro being in the Baroka Valley?"

A voice, tired with age, answered, *"No, there is nothing about Mindoro."*

Suddenly, a stack of books they had not yet examined slid off of the table and clattered to the floor. Deanna turned and noticed that one of the book fairies had grabbed one of the books they had not yet seen and was flying across the room. "Hey!" she shouted. "Come back here with that book." The book fairy hovered twenty feet above the floor, along the far wall.

Derek called the tiny librarian who appeared instantly. She ordered the book fairy to come down at once. The tiny fairy made no move to come down, so the librarian pulled out a wand.

Before the librarian could cast a spell, the book fairy opened its mouth and sent a blast of frozen white breath at them. Deanna shivered uncontrollably, and Derek felt his fingers getting numb.

Deanna thought about using the Book of Spells, but the Wand of Ondarell shook in her hand. She would not be able to aim a spell accurately.

Before she could come up with a plan, she felt something rubbing against her leg. Startled, she looked down and saw a huge black cat nuzzling against her.

"I'll take care of it," the cat purred. Deanna was shocked that the cat spoke, but with her teeth chattering, she could only nod in response.

Derek and Deanna watched as the cat hopped onto the librarian's desk and picked up a roll of tape. He then leapt onto the table directly under the hovering book fairy. He pulled a small bottle of honey from the sack he wore over his shoulder. He squeezed a few drops of honey onto the table and looked up.

The book fairy's eyes widened. The little creature sniffed the air and was overcome by the smell of the honey. It shot down to the table and began to lick at the tiny golden drops.

The cat slapped one of his paws on the book fairy to keep it from escaping and then put a piece of tape across its mouth so that it could not fire more ice breath at him. He then took another piece of tape and taped the book fairy to the table. When he had captured the renegade book fairy, he purred at Deanna.

The librarian hurried over with a spool of

golden thread. She wrapped the fairy in the shimmering thread, pulled it from the table, and carried it into the back room.

Deanna came over and picked up the book. "Thanks," she said to the cat.

"Always glad to help a Mystical Guardian," the cat replied. "My name is Zorell. Anytime you need help, just ask." He curled up in a patch of sunlight shining down from one of the Library's high windows and watched as Derek and Deanna continued their search.

Deanna touched her wand to the book's cover and said, *"Explanatum."* The book shuddered. "Do you know any stories about Mindoro being in the Baroka Valley?" Deanna asked forcefully.

The book's cover flew open and the pages fluttered until they reached page 238. A hushed voice said:

> *Mindoro came to the Baroka Valley 286 years ago and spent three days in the Atteelian Orchard which is guarded by the Armored Giants. As he prepared to leave the Orchard, he was captured by Eldrack. There is no further mention of Mindoro in the Baroka Valley.*

"I guess we're going to the Atteelian Orchard," Derek said. He picked up his backpack and walked to the librarian's desk to tell her that the rest of the books could be returned to their shelves.

A swarm of book fairies shot out from under the librarian's desk and raced to return the books to the towering shelves. Their silvery wings shimmered in the candlelight. They reminded Derek of a cloud of lightning bugs in the backyard during the summer.

Deanna looked down at Zorell and asked, "Do you know how to get to the Goose Lot?"

"Goose Lot, hmm? You're planning to fly first class," the cat replied. "Yes, I know where it is. I'll take you there." Zorell led the way past the librarian's desk out of the library.

"To the Goose Lot," Derek smiled. Deanna and Derek followed the large black cat into the warm Amemnop afternoon.

3 The Goose Takes Flight

Zorell led Derek and Deanna through the winding streets of Amemnop for nearly half an hour before they finally saw an open field in front of them. A huge sign told them that they had reached the "Goose Lot." Near the Goose Lot's office, they could see Tobungus checking a schedule board. He saw them and waved eagerly. He began to run toward them as quickly as his wooden shoes would allow.

Zorell saw Tobungus and stopped. "Surely you're not traveling with him."

"Tobungus?" Deanna replied. "He's our friend and guide. What's wrong with him?"

"He's a lunatic," the cat replied.

"Well, Iszarre trusts him," Derek said. "Tobungus came through with a powerful spell when we were battling Eldrack."

Before Zorell could respond, Tobungus reached them. "Beast!" he called out, pointing at Zorell.

"You see what I'm saying?" Zorell asked.

"Don't act so innocent," Tobungus cut in. "You spent four months treating me like a scratching post."

"And I'll do it again, if you're not careful," Zorell said, hissing as he spoke.

"Settle down, both of you," Deanna said sternly. "We have a bigger problem than your silly argument. We have to get to the Baroka Valley and find the second moonstone. Have you forgotten about Eldrack and his threat to peace in Elestra?"

"You're right," Tobungus agreed, still eyeing Zorell warily. "I've arranged for us to fly on a goose all the way to the entry to the Baroka Valley. We'll have to walk to the Atteelian Orchard from there."

"I'm afraid that I can't go with you," Zorell said to Derek and Deanna. "Cats are not allowed to ride on the geese."

"Gee, I wonder why, you clawed menace," Tobungus said.

"Tobungus," Derek warned, as he moved in between the two "old friends." "This is getting us nowhere."

"Right, I'm sorry," Tobungus said in a dignified voice to Zorell. The cat nodded his head in an equally dignified manner and said goodbye to the three travelers. He turned and headed back into town.

Tobungus led Derek and Deanna over to a bench near a grassy pen where several geese were nibbling on seeds.

Deanna looked confused, and Derek waited for Tobungus to make the next move. They waited awkwardly for five minutes until a tall man wearing a tattered wizard's robe walked over and announced that their goose was just about ready for the flight to the Baroka Valley.

The man led them to a long straight stone path. At the far end, a single goose stood. As they approached the bird, they could not see anything to suggest that it could carry them to the Baroka Valley. It was a regular goose, just like those that they had seen in the park back in their hometown. In fact, it wasn't a particularly big goose. It looked more like a mid-size duck.

The tall man pulled out a wand and said *"Goosio Enlargeum."* The goose began to swell. Within seconds, it was the size of a car. "Climb on," the man said.

Tobungus hopped onto the goose's back and settled comfortably in the soft down. Derek and Deanna reluctantly followed him onboard. At that moment, they were not convinced that goose travel was, as Zorell had put it, "first class."

As soon as they were seated among the enormous white and brown feathers, the goose stood up and began moving down a wide, grassy path which served as a runway. The goose took off and headed into the fluffy clouds overhead.

Derek and Deanna couldn't believe that they were actually flying on a goose. At first, they were nervous about looking down, but they soon realized that a magic spell was holding them in place. A bit more confidently, they looked out over the hills, forests, lakes, and cities of Magia.

The goose soared higher as towering mountains with sharp peaks appeared in front of them. But even at its highest, the goose could not get over the tallest peaks, so it had to fly between the mountains. Deanna struggled to see the tops of the mountains, but saw that they faded into the clouds. Tobungus told them that these were the Bagayama Mountains, the tallest mountains in Magia.

The highest of the Bagayama Mountains reached above Elestra's atmosphere and were completely barren at their uppermost points. Only a few creatures ever ventured to the rocky mountain tops.

After an hour, they had passed the Bagayama Mountains and flew over flat meadows with herds of gigantic animals singing happy-sounding songs in surprisingly high-pitched, whiny voices.

A bit further on, they saw clouds of steam rising from the ground. "That's the River of the Dragon's Breath," Tobungus shouted over the whipping wind. "You'll have to hold on in case the goose has to swerve. The magic may not be enough to keep you on the goose's back."

As they flew into the river's steam, the air around them became misty, and they could not see more than ten feet in front of the goose. Deanna quickly made sure that the Wand of Ondarell was secured tightly in her belt.

They squinted, trying to see the river below them, but they saw only clouds of steam. Without warning, a huge blast of steam shot up in front of them. The goose jerked to the right, just missing the geyser. The goose seemed completely calm in the face of the eruption.

Another blast off to their right forced the goose back to the left. The massive bird swerved in and out of towering columns of blistering steam for nearly five minutes before the river's surface calmed down.

"Just how big is this river?" Derek yelled to Tobungus over the hissing sound of the steam jets behind them.

"The river is over a mile wide in some places," Tobungus replied. "In other places, it is only a hundred feet wide. Now, we're over the middle of the river which is usually calmer."

After several minutes of calm, the goose was forced to swerve to avoid another steam geyser. Once again, the bird zigged and zagged between the blasts of steam. After five more tense minutes, they saw the faint outlines of trees. The fog was becoming thinner. They were reaching the edge of the river.

When the goose finally shot out of the steam clouds, Derek and Deanna felt like cheering in celebration. But, they stayed quiet so that they would not scare the goose. The last thing that they wanted was for the goose to think it had gone the wrong way and turn around to fly back over the river.

"I suppose you see why you have to fly over the river," Tobungus remarked.

"I can't imagine that anyone ever sails on the river," Deanna replied, shaking her head.

"It is possible," Tobungus nodded, "but you would need powerful magic to get past the geysers and through the boiling rapids."

The goose circled a clearing in front of a lush forest before coming to a gentle landing. As soon as the three passengers got off of the bird's back, it shrunk back to its normal size and began nibbling at the grass.

A short woman walked over with a dish of water and said, "Drink up, Goosey. You deserve it." Looking up at the children, she said, "He's got to eat and drink before his next flight. I hope your flight was pleasant."

"Oh, yes," Deanna replied. "It was our first goose flight." They thanked the woman and the goose, and started toward the forest.

The trees in the forest were as tall as skyscrapers, and their lowest branches were as big as normal trees. Derek saw Tobungus staring into the forest. "What's wrong, Tobungus?" he asked.

"Nothing," Tobungus answered. "This is the Forest of Confusion. I once knew what that meant, but I can't remember now. I have a feeling the name is important." He paused in thought. Finally, he sighed and said, "Ah, well, I'm sure we'll figure it out."

4 A Snail's Pace

Derek was growing impatient because Deanna and Tobungus seemed to be dawdling on the path to the Forest of Confusion. Deanna had stopped and opened the magical locket hanging around her neck. She wanted to look in the Book of Spells for anything that mentioned the Forest, and Tobungus decided that he had to stop to change his shoes. Derek felt very small next to the trees that loomed in front of him, and he wanted to get started so that they could get through the forest.

"My feet hurt," Tobungus complained. "Those wooden shoes are very stylish in town and they make a great sound on the boardwalk, but they sure do squish my toes on a long hike."

"Tobungus," Derek began exasperated, "they're wooden shoes. What could possibly make you think that they would be comfortable?" He sensed that Deanna was about to say something, so he turned quickly to her. "And you, Deanna, you're taking forever with the Book of Spells. We need to get through the Forest before Eldrack gets his hands on the second moonstone."

"Derek," Deanna said, "What are the chances that Eldrack knows we're here?"

"Look, Deanna," Derek replied, "Eldrack might not have known we were looking for the first moonstone, when he first learned we were in Elestra, but he sure knows what we're up to now."

"Okay, okay," Deanna said, closing the Book of Spells back into the locket. "The Forest looked pretty small from the air, so we should be able to run through it and find the Atteelian Orchard."

"I'm right behind you," Tobungus said, tying a pair of bright orange running shoes he had selected from his shoe bag. The three of them rushed up the path and saw a short old man sitting on a huge tree stump next to a giant snail.

"Wow," Derek said, "I guess the books were right about everything being huge in the Baroka Valley." The snail was the size of an elephant, but it moved as slowly as a regular garden snail.

When he saw the friends coming, the old man picked up a gnarled walking stick and pushed himself up. He hobbled over to the children and said, "Welcome. Are you looking for a ride through the Forest of Confusion?"

"No, thank you," Deanna replied. "I think we can make it on our own."

"I wouldn't be so sure," the old man said, his dark eyes glittering. "The Forest of Confusion can be . . . confusing."

"Is it dangerous?" Derek asked.

"No, no, it's quite safe, unless you consider the nut-throwing owl sprites," he laughed. "It's just not what you would expect," he added mysteriously.

Derek and Deanna felt confident after finding the first moonstone, and they wanted to conquer the Forest of Confusion on their own. "Thanks again," Deanna said, "but we're going to give it a try by ourselves."

"Very well," the old man said before going back to his stump. "I'll be right here, if you change your minds." He chuckled to himself, knowing that they were not prepared for the Forest of Confusion.

Derek led the way into the Forest. Tobungus and Deanna followed cautiously. They stopped several feet inside the tree line and looked at the path ahead. They could see the far side of the forest peeking through the trees.

They didn't see anything confusing about the Forest of Confusion. The edge of the forest looked like it was no more than three hundred feet in front of them. The forest looked like it was taller than it was long.

Derek looked at Deanna and smiled. "I bet I can beat you to the other side," he said.

"You're on," Deanna replied.

Before they could start running, Tobungus shot past them calling out, "You can't beat a fungus! Especially if he cheats!"

They took off after the laughing mushroom man. Derek caught Tobungus, but then Deanna pulled into the lead. Laughing, they went back and forth for nearly fifteen minutes, without checking on their progress through the forest.

They all stopped at the same time. They were tired and panting hard. Deanna looked down the path and saw the edge of the Forest, but it still seemed to be three hundred feet away. "What's going on?" she asked.

Derek looked behind them and noticed that they were still near the entrance to the Forest. "How can we be back here?" he added.

"Maybe we went around in a circle," Tobungus suggested.

Deanna shook her head. "The path was straight," she replied. "Let's keep walking and check our progress again in a few minutes."

They walked for five minutes before looking back. They were still near the Forest's entrance, and they had only moved two or three feet. "I don't get this," Derek said.

"It is called the Forest of Confusion after all," Deanna mused. Before she could say anything else, something hit her on the head. "Ow," she said, looking up.

Above them, there were dozens of tiny, human-faced owls with long narrow noses flying among the lower branches of the forest's huge trees. "Those must be the owl sprites," Derek said. One of the tiny owl sprites threw a wrinkly, tan nut at him, and as he jumped out of the way, it hit Tobungus on the arm.

"Hey," Tobungus said. "What's the big idea?"

"Hee hee," another owl sprite laughed. "Catch this one." It threw another nut which hit Derek in the leg. A wave of nuts rained down on them, forcing them to scatter for a few seconds.

"Stop throwing those nuts at us," Deanna called.

"Okay!" one of the owl sprites giggled as it

threw another nut.

After another minute of dodging the falling nuts, Deanna finally said, "Fine! Go ahead. See if I care. Throw the nuts at us." The owl sprites landed on the trees' branches and stopped throwing the nuts.

Amazed, Derek and Deanna looked up at the sprites. Derek thought for a few seconds. "I've got it," he said. "Everything's opposite here."

"What do you mean?" Deanna asked.

"It's simple," Derek said. "You told the sprites to stop throwing nuts, and they didn't. But, when you told them not to stop, they stopped. Make sense?"

"If you say so," replied Deanna.

"I bet that means," Derek continued excitedly as if Deanna hadn't interrupted him, "We need to go very slowly to get through the Forest. We need to go slowly to travel a short distance quickly."

"That's it!" Tobungus shouted. "To make it through the Forest, we would have to walk for days, even at our slowest pace."

"Yep," Derek said, nodding. "We were trying to run, but we were getting nowhere."

"That's the reason that they have the snail-drawn carriages outside the Forest," Tobungus said. "The snails are the only creatures that can move slowly enough to get you through the Forest quickly."

"That makes no sense," Deanna said.

"Of course not," Tobungus agreed cheerfully. "It's the Forest of Confusion."

They left the Forest and walked back to the old man. He looked as if he had expected them to return. "Have you come back for a snail ride?"

"It looks that way," Derek said smiling. "We nearly wore ourselves out running through the Forest. It looks like we need to move slowly to get to the other side."

"Yes," the old man nodded approvingly, "that's the key to the Forest. I'll get the carriage hooked up." He hobbled over to the snail and used his wand to bring a four-wheeled carriage up behind it.

Once the carriage was strapped in place, he waved the passengers over and climbed into the front seat. The sun was getting low in the afternoon sky, and Deanna began to worry that they would have to find somewhere to sleep for the night.

It took the snail ten minutes to get into the Forest, and once it was on the path, it slowed down even more. Derek and Deanna looked out of the carriage and were amazed to see the trees zipping by around them. The forest was whizzing by so quickly that they had trouble seeing each individual tree.

Almost before they had settled in, the snail emerged from the far side of the Forest. They immediately noticed that the sun was on the opposite side of the sky, as if it was just coming up. The sky was cloudier than when they entered the forest as well.

The old man noticed their looks of confusion and smiled, "The trip took three minutes for us, but outside the Forest, sixteen hours passed. It is morning now, so you have the whole day ahead of you."

"This is incredible," Deanna said to the old man. "If you don't mind my asking, do you know how to get to the Atteelian Orchard from here?" She wanted to make sure that they did not waste any more time just because they didn't stop to ask for directions. Derek's reminder that Eldrack might be trying to find the second moonstone too made Deanna feel like they needed to find the Orchard as quickly as possible.

"The Atteelian Orchard lies beyond the Dryggian Beach, past the Rhodian Flatlands, and over the Plendarr Hills," he replied. "This path ends at the Dryggian Beach, so you'll have to walk along the shore until you see a sign for the Rhodian Flatlands. I'll warn you that it will take a while to get past the sand on the beach. When you get past the Flatlands, you will see Tull's Magic Shop. Take the path that goes to the right and cross the bubbling creek. The path will take you through the Plendarr Hills and right to the Orchard."

Tobungus changed into hiking boots for the next part of their journey. Derek and Deanna thanked the old man, and they headed down the path to the Dryggian Beach, thinking that it would be nice to take off their shoes and walk in the wet sand of the beach.

After an hour of walking along the path, they saw a sign that said "Welcome to the Dryggian Beach. Please do not remove the grains of sand!"

"How predictably weird," Deanna said.

Derek nodded his agreement and walked past the sign. Soon, they saw why the sign mentioned individual grains of sand. The beach was a collection of two foot wide sand boulders.

Derek and Deanna climbed onto one of the sandy rocks and looked out over the lake. A fish the size of a bus jumped out of the water and grabbed a dragonfly that looked like it could carry a whole family of people across the lake. They stood mesmerized as they watched the giant creatures of the lake.

Their fascination was broken by the baritone croaking of a six foot wide frog off to their left. "I think we'd better get moving," Derek said. "Who knows what types of dangerous creatures might be lurking around here."

Deanna agreed. They hopped from sand grain to sand grain, with Tobungus bringing up the rear.

"Not exactly a relaxing day at the beach," Deanna said as they finally got past the beach and walked along the path to the Rhodian Flat Lands.

"Listen, Daring and Dino," Tobungus said, "I know that we have to keep moving, but I have to stop for a few minutes. Climbing over those rocks killed my feet."

"You know, Dino," Derek said, "For once I agree with Tobumpus, even if he can't remember our names."

"Hey," Tobungus said, "what's so hard about the name Tobungus?"

Derek and Deanna looked at each other

and laughed. "Deanna, do you know a spell to conjure up some food for us?" Derek asked. "I'm starved."

"No," Deanna replied. "That would be a nice spell to learn, though. I could try to find one in the Book of Spells."

"I've got it covered," Tobungus said. He slid his minimizing bag from his shoulder and nearly dove inside. After a few moments, he emerged with a bag of food that Glabber had given him for their trip.

"Let's see," Tobungus said, reaching inside the food bag. He pulled out a handful of rocks of various colors. "Okay, we have some sort of sandwiches, blarr fruit, and shaken milk."

"Do you mean milkshake?" Deanna asked.

"Oh, yes, I guess that's it," Tobungus replied, looking at three brownish stones.

"Wait a second, Tobungus," Derek said. "Those are rocks, not food. How do you expect us to eat that?"

"Glabber put a food bag spell on the food," Tobungus explained. "Here, look." He pulled out a small jar that resembled a salt shaker and sprinkled a few sparkling grains on each rock. Instantly, the rocks began to tremble and then transformed into a full meal of sandwiches, fruit, and chocolate milkshakes.

"That's more like it," Derek said, grabbing a sandwich and milkshake.

"Amazing," is all that Deanna could say.

They sat in the grass to eat, while Tobungus told them that turning the food into rocks was an excellent way to protect it while traveling. He also said that he had enough food for three days, but that they could stop and pick up more along the way if necessary.

They ate quickly and laid back in the grass to give their legs a few more minutes of rest before continuing on their journey.

5 Green Thumb

After their break was over, Derek, Deanna, and Tobungus started walking along the path. Before long, they came to a worn wooden sign that said:

Welcome to the Rhodian Flatlands.
Don't wear yellow and please do not
feed the wild chickens.

Derek looked at Tobungus. "You're from here, aren't you, Tobungus?" he asked.

"No, I've never been here before," Tobungus replied a bit surprised. "Why would you think I come from this area?"

"That sign seems just about as weird as you," Derek said laughing.

"Very funny, Hambone," Tobungus replied. "For your information, I am from the Torrallian Forest."

"Well, I'm sure it's a very nice place," Deanna began, "but do you two think you can make it through the Flatlands without teasing each other?" It was her turn to be impatient. She walked past the sign and waved for the others to follow her.

"You're right," Derek said. "We should be watching for signs of danger as we get closer to the orchard."

After a few minutes, they saw something large and reddish-brown well off of the path to their left. As they walked on, they realized that it was a giant chicken running toward them. The ground shook as the huge bird stomped along. The chicken stopped less than twenty feet from the path and began eating a patch of huge yellow flowers.

Derek pointed to the yellow flowers that the chicken was devouring. "That's probably the reason that sign said not to wear yellow," he said, relieved that they had not just become chicken squish. "Somebody wearing yellow would be about the same size as those flowers."

"You see," Tobungus said loudly, "the sign wasn't so weird after all."

The chicken looked up at the sound of Tobungus' voice. "Shh!" Derek whispered. They stood absolutely still and waited for the chicken to turn back to its meal of yellow flowers.

They all let out sighs of relief when the chicken lowered its head and began eating again. They walked quickly and quietly further down the path, keeping an eye out for other giant creatures along the way.

The next twenty minutes went by without interruption from giant chickens, exploding rivers, or nut-throwing owl sprites. But just when they were starting to relax and enjoy the scenery, their peaceful walk was suddenly disrupted by a three foot tall creature with green skin and a brown cape.

He held up his hand as they approached and said, "Where do you think you're going?"

"We're going to the other side of the Rhodian Flatlands," Derek replied.

"That seems pretty obvious," the little man said, eyeing them suspiciously. "Where are you going after you leave the Flatlands?"

"We're headed to the Atteelian Orchard," Derek shot back.

"Derek!" Deanna said, thinking that they should keep their plans secret.

"So, you're Derek, the new Guardian" the little man said with a nasty, yellow-toothed smile. "My master will be pleased that I have stopped you along your way."

"What master?   Who are you?" Deanna asked.

"And how do you know about me?" Derek added.

"My name is The Great, Powerful, Wise, Talented, Stylish, Handsome, Clever, Intelligent, Funny Green Thumb, but you can simply call me Green Thumb when you tell Eldrack who captured you," the little man said proudly. "As a magnificent forest elf, I use my power over Elestra's plants to assist my master Eldrack."

Deanna looked around nervously, wondering whether Eldrack was nearby. Fortunately, she saw nobody except the odd green forest elf. "There's only one of you," she observed, "and three of us, so I think we'll go on our way."

"You are mistaken, little lady," the forest elf said. "I am not alone. I have the plant life of Elestra on my side."

Derek looked down and chuckled. "I'm pretty sure that the grass here in the Flatlands won't stop us."

"Yes, I see your point," the forest elf said with a wicked glint in his beady little eyes, "the grass is a weak ally. A thorn-covered tree would be so much better." He bent down and touched his oversized thumb to the ground. The field rumbled and seconds later, a tree sprouted and grew to forty feet tall almost instantly. "As you can see," he said, "I have more powerful plant friends than the grass."

Deanna stepped behind Tobungus and opened the charm with the Book of Spells on her necklace. She found a spell that sounded promising. She stepped out into the open and said, "Your simple tricks will not stop us. You can step aside, or I will have to remove your little tree."

Green Thumb was dancing around, singing "I'm so great! I'm so great!" but stopped after a third "I'm so," to reply to Deanna. "Young lady," the forest elf said threateningly, "I don't know how you intend to battle my magic, but you should know that you cannot win. As the song says, 'I'm so great.'"

"Enough talking," Deanna said.

"And singing," Tobungus murmured behind her.

"Not to mention that awful dancing," Derek whispered to Tobungus.

Deanna pulled out the Wand of Ondarell and pointed it at the thorny tree. "*Cyclonicus*," she yelled, pointing the wand at the tree. The tree began to spin. It spun faster and faster and finally was sucked into the ground like soda through a straw.

Green Thumb looked shocked that someone could remove one of his creations so quickly.

Derek and Tobungus started to walk forward, but they stopped when they saw the forest elf hold up both thumbs and then bend down. This time, he touched both hands to the ground and two new trees popped up. The quickly rising trees knocked Derek to the ground, but he jumped up and dusted himself off.

Deanna repeated her spell at each tree and once again the trees spun in a whirlwind and disappeared into the ground. The elf growled in frustration and quickly pressed his thumbs to the ground making two more trees appear, then two more, and then two more after that. Soon, it was a battle of speed between the forest elf's Green Thumb spell and Deanna's *Cyclonicus* spell.

Derek saw that Deanna was falling behind. The forest elf was able to use both of his thumbs and make two trees appear in the time that Deanna could make one disappear. He looked around, trying to find some way to get past the forest elf who claimed to have all plant life on his side.

Derek didn't realize he had gotten too close to Green Thumb. Suddenly, a tree sprouted from the ground beneath his feet. He was carried high into the air on the thorny branches of the swaying tree.

Derek held on tight while he tried to concentrate on finding a way to stop Green Thumb. Suddenly, he saw the answer. "Deanna," he called down excitedly, "if he can use the plants, then we have to use the animals."

Deanna looked confused, so Derek pointed back at the giant chicken standing well behind them. "Use the spell that changes the color of clothes."

Deanna instantly understood Derek's plan. She reached into her backpack and pulled out her gray T-shirt. She touched the wand to it and said, "*Colorum clotharro yellow*," and watched as the shirt turned yellow.

She threw the shirt up in the air and shouted "*Levitato*," as she pointed the wand at it. The shirt fluttered in the air and then moved wherever the wand directed it. She waved the shirt high in the air in front of the chicken. The chicken saw the yellow target and began running toward it, leaving its meal of yellow flowers behind.

Deanna guided the shirt toward the forest elf. When the chicken was only twenty feet away, she used the color spell on the little elf's cape. She changed her shirt back to gray, guided it back to her, and put it back in her backpack. When the chicken saw the elf's flowing yellow cape, he charged toward it.

Green Thumb turned when he heard the mad clucking of the chicken. His eyes widened as he saw the enormous chicken crashing towards him through the thorny trees. Red feathers, the size of kites were flying everywhere.

Deanna quickly used a shield spell to deflect trees that were flying around after being snapped like twigs by the chicken.

Deanna used the *Levitato* spell on Derek and brought him back to the ground safely. "Nice job, Deanna," Derek said, as trees bounced off of the glowing shield that arched over them.

The forest elf shouted angrily and spun around and ran, leaving the children free to continue their journey.

Derek and Deanna watched as the forest elf tried to make trees to block the chicken's path. The chicken was so large that it was able to stomp on the trees as they sprouted from the ground.

"The sign warned you not to wear yellow," Tobungus called after the forest elf. Turning to Deanna, he said, "Soon we will have to give you the title Ham if your magical ability continues to grow."

"Tobungus, she's been a ham all her life," Derek said laughing.

"Ha, ha," Deanna said. "It's ironic that the smallest creature we've seen in the Baroka Valley has given us the greatest amount of trouble. We'd better be careful if Eldrack has any huge beasts on his side here."

"You know, Deanna," Derek said seriously, "I should have told you to use the *Cyclonicus* spell on Green Thumb instead of the trees. That would have solved our problems much faster."

"Well, I got the chance to practice with the wand a lot more," she said, surprised that he sounded so disappointed in himself.

"I guess you're right," Derek said. "The better you get with that wand, the easier it will be to defeat Eldrack."

"Besides, you came up with a really good idea when you were up in the tree," Deanna replied, trying to cheer him up. "I don't think I would have been thinking clearly if a mutant thorny tree had whisked me up into the air."

"Yeah, but next time it may be Eldrack instead of Green Thumb," Derek said. "And, Eldrack's way more powerful.

"Derek, your idea is what beat Green Thumb," Deanna said, putting the wand back in her pack. "Come on, let's go."

She didn't notice that Derek had dropped a few steps behind her and looked very impressed, if not a little intimidated, by the way she had used the wand against Green Thumb.

6 Tull's Magic Shop

Deanna, Derek, and Tobungus moved quickly along the path and were happy to see a sign telling them that they were leaving the Rhodian Flatlands. Seeing Green Thumb confirmed that Eldrack knew they were in the Baroka Valley, so they wanted to get to the Atteelian Orchard as quickly as possible. After a few minutes of walking, they saw a tiny hut with ragged wood walls and a rounded grass roof. A sign above the hut's only door said "Tull's Magic Shop."

Derek said, "We know we're going the right way at least. We should reach the Plendarr Hills around the next bend."

"Wait," Deanna stopped. "Let's go into the magic shop. Who knows what we'll find."

"Ooh," Tobungus said excitedly, pushing past Derek. "They might have more lemons, or limes, or maybe, dare I dream it, grapefruit."

"Well, maybe they would have a wand

that I could actually use," Derek said half-jokingly.

"You want the wand?" Deanna asked surprised. She pulled the wand out of her pack and shoved it in his hand. "Here, you take it for a while."

"What am I supposed to do with it?" Derek asked.

"I don't know, but it's important that you get some practice too," Deanna replied. "Why don't you change the color of your clothes."

"Okay," Derek said, "sounds easy enough. I think I'll turn my shirt blue."

He turned the wand toward his chest and touched the tip to his shirt. "*Colorum clotharro*," he said loudly. Sparks shot from the end of the wand and he felt his shirt sizzle.

"Not quite," Deanna laughed. Derek looked down and saw that his shirt had turned bright pink with yellow spots. "You have to say the color you want, or the wand picks a random color," she said.

Derek put his hand on his stomach and touched the wand to his shirt. He didn't notice that the tip was barely grazing his other hand. "*Colorum clotharro blue*," he said.

His shirt sizzled, but then he felt a

sensation like warm goose bumps wash over his skin.

"Looking good, Bluebird," Tobungus said before falling down in laughter.

Derek looked down at his hands and saw that they were bright blue. "Deanna?" he said nervously.

"Well, you got the right color this time," she said as she cracked up. "Blue shirt, blue skin. Very monochromatic."

"Deanna, how do I reverse it?" Derek said in a panic and thrust the wand back into her hand.

"Don't worry," Deanna said. "We'll find the counterspell." She sat down in the shaggy grass and opened the Book of Spells. She read through the long list of spells in the table of contents, but could not find anything that would change the color of Derek's skin. "I'm sorry, Derek," she sighed finally. "I can't find anything to help you in the book. I can change you to a different color, but I can't make the color go away. Maybe we should try the magic shop."

"Yeah, they probably would know what to do," he said hopefully.

"We could leave you this way and give you the title, Derek the Blue," Tobungus joked.

Seeing Derek's frustrated expression, he added, "No, well, perhaps after we find all of the moonstones, you can choose a nice color."

Deanna led the way into Tull's Magic Shop. They walked through the door and found themselves in a gigantic room. All three looked around, amazed at the immense size of the inside of the hut. "How is this possible?" Deanna whispered.

"Magic," a flat voice said. "I am Tull, and this is a magic shop, so I can use magic to make my shop grow. A large shop is important, given the size of some of my visitors from the Baroka Valley."

Tull stood behind a thick wooden counter lined with huge glass jars filled with swimming creatures, dried roots, and colorful balls of glass. Even in the dim light that oozed through the Magic Shop's small windows, his golden eyes shimmered.

"Fascinating," Deanna said looking around. Derek elbowed her in the side to remind her why they were there. "Oh, yes. We're looking for something to help my brother."

Tull came out from behind the counter, circled Derek, and looked him up and down. "Yes, I see. He's a bit short. He needs to grow a foot or two," he concluded.

"No, that's not it," Deanna replied.

Before she could go on, Tull cut in, "Then it must be his nose. He only has one, and that one's pretty small. Well, we can fix him up with a nice snout."

"No," Deanna said, trying not to laugh, "don't you see anything else wrong with him."

"Let's see," Tull said, taking a closer look. "Bad breath? Dirty finger nails? Dry elbows? Bad breath?"

"Hey," Derek said, "you said that one already."

"Hmm," the shopkeeper replied, "then it must be really bad."

"No," Derek shouted, "I'm blue."

"And a beautiful shade of blue you are," Tull exclaimed. He waited for Derek to say something, but saw that he was staring up at the ceiling. "Oh, you don't want to be blue." He patted Derek on the shoulder. "Sit down on the big red cushion near the wall and I'll make you a potion."

"It's not going to have eye of newt or wings of a bat in it? Is it?" Derek asked more nervous now than he was when he first realized he had turned himself blue.

"That's disgusting," Tull said. "This potion will have all sorts of normal food." He opened a wooden door on a cupboard and pulled out a glass, a pitcher of milk, a small bottle of a red sauce, an onion, and a salt shaker. He poured a glass of milk and then added several shakes of salt and the entire onion. Finally, he dumped an overflowing spoonful of the red sauce into the milky mixture. As the red sauce dripped into the glass, Derek could see that it was smoking.

"Here we go," Tull said, "it's finished."

"I can't drink that," Derek said, "I'll get sick."

"You don't drink all potions, young man," Tull replied. He poured the glass of white potion into a pot of soil next to his work table. Within seconds, two leaves popped out from the soil. Before long, Derek could see a miniature tree rising out of the soil. Finally, the tree stopped growing and a single yellow lemon hung from one of the branches. The lemon was no bigger than a pea. Tull picked it carefully with two fingers.

"You will have to eat this lemon," Tull announced. "It will erase the magic that made you blue."

Derek popped the tiny yellow fruit into his

mouth, chewed twice, and swallowed. He felt goose bumps rush down his arms a second time, but this time, they were cold. He looked at his hands and saw that the blue was fading. Finally, his hands returned to their normal color. "Thank you," Derek said sincerely.

"It is my pleasure to help children who wish to become wizards," Tull replied. "Is there anything you are looking for in my shop."

"Not really, "Deanna said. "We're on a journey and we were hoping that we might find some magical items to help us on our way."

"You should probably wait until you're older to learn magic," Tull chuckled.

"It's not that easy," Deanna replied. "We're Mystical Guardians and we have to learn as much magic as we can." *As quickly as we can*, she thought to herself.

Tull's golden eyes widened. "My, oh my…Oh, I had no idea…Oh my," Tull stammered. "For many years, my family has been waiting for you to come."

"What are you talking about?" Derek asked.

"When I was young, my father told me a legend about a huge battle between good and evil. The Mystical Guardians were fighting a force of powerful creatures led by an evil wizard."

"That sounds like our family against Eldrack," Deanna said. "When did this battle happen?"

"It hasn't happened yet," Tull said. "The legend said that the evil wizard would build his power as the new Mystical Guardians began their struggle to stop him."

"That doesn't sound good," Derek muttered. "Why has your family been waiting for us?"

"Ah," Tull said, "Come with me. I have something for you." He led Derek, Deanna, and Tobungus down a narrow hallway behind the counter.

They wound around the passage for several minutes before coming to a steep staircase heading down into a dark basement. Tull picked up a torch and walked into the darkness.

"What exactly are we doing back here?" Tobungus whispered nervously to Deanna.

"Just come on," Deanna said in a hushed voice, "Tull has something to show us."

At the foot of the stairs, they found themselves in a small room that looked like a damp cave. They walked over to the wall where

Tull was standing. There, sitting on a small ledge was an orange monkey. "What's going on?" Derek asked, looking from the orange monkey to Tull and back to the orange monkey again.

"There's something that we've been guarding for a long time," Tull began. "We were instructed to give it only to Mystical Guardians, and now that you're here, we can be done with it."

Turning to the monkey, he said, "these children are the new Mystical Guardians, so we can give them the scroll and the key."

"How do we know that they're Mystical Guardians?" the monkey challenged.

"You smelly little monkey, just give me the key," Tull snapped.

"I've been sitting down in this stinking hole in the ground for years, hoping to see the Mystical Guardians, and now two children come," the monkey said.

Deanna was about to say something, but the monkey cut her off.

"I always expected some wise old wizard with flowing robes and a long white beard," the monkey said stubbornly. "I'm not sure that I can believe that these children are Mystical Guardians. I will need proof."

Tull and the monkey continued arguing. Deanna pulled out the Wand of Ondarell. "This should be proof enough," she said. "It is the Wand of Ondarell. This wand was given to us by our grandfather, Phillipe the Brave, the thirteenth Mystical Guardian. We have already completed a quest set in motion by Baladorn, the first Mystical Guardian. Now we are racing to complete our second quest." A magical wind blew through the cave as she said these words. Tull and the monkey fell silent.

"Then you are who you say you are," the monkey said in awe. He bowed and moved aside to reveal a shallow nook in the wall where a shining gold key was hidden. Derek removed the key and asked, "What is this for?"

"We're not sure," Tull replied nervously. "All we know is that we were supposed to protect it until the Mystical Guardians arrived."

"Well, we'll try to find the lock that it fits," Deanna said. She put the key carefully into her pocket.

Tull pressed a rocky knob next to the key's nook and a small door opened. Inside was a tattered tan scroll. He took it out and handed it to Deanna. "This scroll should help you on your way," he said.

The monkey jumped onto Tull's shoulder, eager to be freed from his guard duty. They walked back upstairs and thanked Tull again before heading back to the path that led into the Plendarr Hills.

"I wish you good luck," Tull said before they left. "Remember that you are in the Baroka Valley, so things that are usually small and harmless may end up being large and, well, harmful."

"We won't forget that, after seeing the monster chicken rampaging across the Rhodian Flatlands," Derek said. "And the snail that pulled the carriage through the Forest of Confusion, it was the size of a bus."

"Yeah, and climbing the giant grains of sand was a tiring reminder of the size of everything here," Tobungus added.

"Well, it seems like you're getting used to the Baroka Valley," Tull said, chuckling as he followed them through the door.

Once they were out of the dimly lit magic shop, Tull said, "I think I'll let the monkey sit in the sun for a while. His time in that basement was a bit much, especially for an ornery monkey."

The monkey stretched out in the grass

with his belly pointing up toward the sky, as if he couldn't agree more.

7 The Atteelian Orchard

Derek, Deanna, and Tobungus waved goodbye and headed down the path that led to the Atteelian Orchard. Once they were away from the Magic Shop, Deanna stopped to read the scroll. She unrolled it and read out loud:

> *Among the fruit of the Atteelian Orchard, where the sun shines in many colors, you will find the moonstone.*

The three friends stared at each other, hoping that one of them knew the answer to their latest puzzle. Tobungus shrugged and continued down the path.

Deanna followed, repeating the scroll's one sentence three times under her breath, trying to figure out what it meant. She remembered the riddle about the dew in the forest where they met Aramaltus on their first night in Amemnop and wondered if she would need to find a spell to help solve the riddle.

Derek muttered about the scientific properties of the color of sunlight, but could think of no possible solution. He wondered whether the type of fruit in the orchard was important. He was thinking that there might be a multicolored fruit that they would see in the sunlight.

Finally, they decided to try to figure out the riddle once they had a chance to look around. After a few hours of walking through the gently rolling Plendarr Hills, they came to a large wooden sign that announced their arrival at the Atteelian Orchard.

"Those must be the Armored Giants," Derek said, pointing to two statues that stood silently on either side of the entrance and that stretched twenty feet into the air. They weren't made of stone, like other statues they had seen. These statues had huge tree trunks for legs, and their arms were thick branches. They had light green chain mail over their brown, wooden heads and wore dark green tunics. Both held enormous shields and swords with eight foot long blades.

As they were about to enter the orchard, the Armored Giant on the right held his sword across the path to block their way.

"What are you doing?" the other Armored Giant boomed.

"All visitors must state their business," the

first said.

"Don't be a fool," the second statue replied. "They are Mystical Guardians. The girl has the Wand that the other Guardians have had."

"Oh, terribly sorry," the first statue said. "Please, be our guests in the Atteelian Orchard."

"Thank you," Deanna said.

"Wait a minute," Derek said, grabbing Deanna's elbow to stop her. "Excuse me, Armored Giants. Which of the other Guardians have come here?"

The statue that had tried to block them wanted to be extra helpful so he quickly said, "We don't know all of their names, but there have been seven Guardians who have come here before you. One of them was a bit orange-ish. That much I do remember."

"And one of them kept scratching his stomach," the other statue added, not wanting to disappoint the Mystical Guardians. "I'm afraid that we can't tell you anything else."

"You have told us a lot," Deanna reassured them. She looked over at Derek to see if he remembered the Mystical Guardians they had seen in the Cave of Imprisonment who fit those descriptions. His smile told her he did.

"Thanks again," Deanna said. They passed the statues and headed into the orchard.

They walked along the path leading into the orchard and saw giant fruit trees rising high into the sky all around them. The tops of many of the trees were hidden in the clouds. They felt tiny next to the trees that made the Armored Giants seem small.

They were so surprised by the size of the trees and the fruit hanging from their branches that they missed a large red bird hovering ten feet to their right.

"Do you need a guide?" the bird chirped.

Before Derek or Deanna could respond, Tobungus called, "What type of bird are you?"

"I am a Goma Bird," the bird chirped happily. "Why do you ask?"

"I notice that you are red and I want to be sure you are not a Pecking Drill Bird." Turning to Derek and Deanna, he said, "Drill Birds are wicked red birds that love to peck at people's noses and ears."

"We would be happy to have you as our guide," Deanna assured the bird. "What can you tell us about the orchard?"

"The Atteelian Orchard is home to over ninety types of fruit," the Goma Bird said.

"There are two villages of dirt-diggers and fruit-pickers in the orchard. These groups are gnomes and elves who do nothing but work around the orchard's trees. The small planting sheds that you'll see throughout the orchard belong to them. In the tops of certain trees, there are small villages of bee-tenders, a group of fairies who train the bees to pollinate the fruit blossoms."

"It sounds very interesting," Deanna said. "Let's walk along the path, and you can tell us what we're seeing."

As they walked along, the Goma Bird happily pointed out various types of trees, as well as dozens of types of grass. Just beyond the entrance to the orchard, they came to a row of vines with red berries the size of basketballs sagging toward the ground. "These are friddleberries," the Goma Bird said. "Each berry holds enough juice for an entire family's meal."

"That's amazing," Derek said. "I wish we had time to try one of those."

"Yes, well, you have to be careful with the friddleberries here," the Goma Bird said. "The bees get a little wild when they smell friddleberry juice."

They walked further into the orchard and saw long swollen fruits hanging from a patch of trees to their left. "Over there, we have Slugfruit," the Goma Bird said, pointing a wing at the green fruit with a single yellow stripe. "Most people don't like it because it's slimy, and the inside of the fruit is a salty, gray goo."

"Then why do they grow it here?" Derek asked.

"Some species love Slugfruit," the Goma Bird said. "Most of the Slugfruit grown here is sent to the Floddan area."

"What type of creature would possibly like something so disgusting?" Derek asked.

"The Floddan Gong Beaters love Slugfruit. They actually have Slugfruit parties where they bake salty Slugfruit pies during the hot summer months," the bird answered.

Next they saw Nobbly Dujinks, a type of spiky yellow fruit that could be used in cakes or as weapons. Tobungus shuddered at the idea of biting into the sharp Dujink spikes.

A noise to their right drew their attention to two elves sawing through the six inch thick stem of a round, rough-skinned fruit that looked like a giant grapefruit. When the stem was cut, the fruit fell to the ground with a thud that shook the whole orchard and rolled down the hill to a pile of similar fruit.

"Imagine how much citrus magic is in one of those," Tobungus said in awe.

"I wouldn't want to get in the way of that thing rumbling down the hill," Derek said. Deanna just shook her head at the huge fruit.

The Goma Bird flew ahead of them describing so many types of fruits that soon, they found it hard to remember each one.

After a while, they reached the top of a small hill and saw a series of huge wooden structures rising thirty feet into the air. "What are those?" Deanna asked.

"Those are the bee hives that house the orchard's bees."

"Bees?" Derek shouted, thinking that the bees living in the hives must be huge.

Without thinking, Deanna pulled the wand out and held it by her side.

The Goma Bird saw the frightened expressions on the children's faces and realized they were imagining eagle-sized bees swooping out of the sky. "Don't worry. The bees are harmless, unless you're covered in friddleberry juice. Their favorite nectar comes from the friddleberry flowers, you see. They leave the hives to feed on the nectar and then go right back to the hives."

"Well, I still want to steer clear of eagle-sized bees," Derek said. The group tiptoed up the path past the bee hives. "We need to start trying to figure out where the moonstone is," Derek whispered to Deanna after a few minutes.

"There are lots of colors here," Deanna observed. "Maybe there's a spot where the sun shines on a bunch of different fruits."

"That's what I thought too," Derek said.

Pointing further down the path, she said, "Tobungus and I will look in that direction. Derek, you look back down the path."

Derek scanned the area behind them and froze. He grabbed Deanna and started pulling her up the path, deeper into the orchard. "What's going on?" she asked.

He pointed behind them and said, "It's Eldrack."

8 A Fruitful Search

Deanna saw Eldrack's long black cloak flowing behind him as he rushed up the path toward them. She turned and ran with Derek and Tobungus as fast as she could up and over a small hill that was covered with trees. As they went down the back side of the hill and out of Eldrack's eyesight, Deanna saw a planting shed off to their right. She ran toward the shed and motioned to Derek and Tobungus to follow her. They ran behind the shed and hid near a group of bushes. The Goma Bird had sensed that there was trouble and had flown off into the trees.

Derek looked up at the shed and noticed that it was a worn wooden building with yellow windows. There was only one door, and Derek did not want to get caught inside a building with no chance of escape.

Deanna opened the charm and the Book of Spells and tried to find a spell that she might use against Eldrack. They were alone without any way to contact Iszarre. She couldn't find anything strong enough to slow down such a powerful wizard.

"Hurry up, Deanna," Derek whispered. Turning to Tobungus, he said, "Can any of these fruits be used like your lemon?"

"No, only citrus fruits contain magic," Tobungus replied. "I could try to use my lemon, but I don't think it would do much good in this wide open area."

"The fruits," Deanna said suddenly. Seeing the confused looks on Derek's and Tobungus' faces, she added, "I have an idea how we can use the fruits. Follow me." She crept along the line of bushes and snuck into the tree line behind Eldrack.

Derek and Tobungus had no idea what Deanna was planning, but they followed her and tried to stay as quiet as possible. Derek looked around, trying to find a safe hiding place, but he saw nothing other than a second planting shed and the bee hives. The planting shed was just like the first, except that its windows were green.

"Okay," Deanna began, "we need to circle around the bee hives so that they are between Eldrack and us." She crept along the line of trees and hoped that Eldrack was still looking for them further along the path. When they were back on the opposite side of the bee hives, she told the others to duck down and wait.

Derek looked up and saw several swollen Slugfruits hanging over them. A few of the slimy blobs were dripping a thick goo on them. "This is a pretty disgusting place to hide, Deanna," he complained.

"Don't worry," Deanna said, "the bees don't like Slugfruit."

"That's reassuring," Derek muttered under his breath.

"Where are you?" an angry voice bellowed. Eldrack was coming back toward their hiding place, but he was unaware of their exact location. A few seconds later, Eldrack appeared over the hill. He was twenty feet from the friddleberry vines and just beyond the bee hives. He stopped and looked carefully for any sign of Derek or Deanna.

Deanna raised the Wand of Ondarell and pointed it at the friddleberry vines. "*Quakus,*" she said softly. The friddleberry vines shook and rattled, as if someone was trying to sneak through them.

"Aha," Eldrack yelled. "I have you now." He rushed to the friddleberry vines and began to search for the children.

"Derek," Deanna whispered, "You're going to have to wake the bees in a minute."

"What? Wake the bees?" Derek sputtered. "Why would I want to wake a swarm of mutant bees?"

"Just trust me," Deanna said, concentrating on Eldrack.

"How am I supposed to wake a swarm of mutant bees?" Derek muttered.

"Iszarre said you were clever, so I'm sure you'll figure something out," she teased.

"You can use my lemon," Tobungus offered tentatively.

"Am I supposed to throw a lemon at those huge beehives?" Derek asked. Then he realized that he had a better idea. "Tobungus, save your lemon. Help me find some rocks." They searched around the ground and began to pile all of the loose rocks they could find near their hiding place.

Deanna raised the wand again, this time aiming it at the friddleberry vines. "*Explosio,*" she said loudly.

Eldrack twirled around at the sound of her voice, just as two friddleberries next to him exploded. A few drops of friddleberry juice splashed onto his shirt. He looked irritated as he raised his wand and said, "This is how you do it. *Explosio!*"

A thin beam of orange light and sparks shot from Eldrack's wand. One of the slugfruits above their heads exploded with a mighty roar, spraying a sickening gray goop all over Tobungus.

"Ugh!" Tobungus groaned.

"Thanks for the tip," Deanna called. "*EXPLOSIO!*" she yelled as loudly as she could. A shower of pink and purple sparks shot from her wand and made five huge friddleberries explode. She repeated the spell four times, sending a shower of friddleberry juice at Eldrack. He was soaked from head to toe. "Derek," she whispered, "It's time to wake the bees."

Derek stood up and threw a walnut-sized rock at the middle bee hive. He then threw a golf ball-sized rock at the farthest hive. Finally, he threw a lemon-sized rock at the nearest hive. Seconds later, they heard a deafening buzzing as dozens of bees flew out of their wooden homes.

Instinctively, Derek ducked back down under the Slugfruit, but the bees did not even notice him. Deanna had been right. The bees did not like the slugfruit. The bees sensed the sweet friddleberry juice covering Eldrack. The swarm headed in his direction, buzzing excitedly.

Eldrack tried to use magic spells to knock

the bees away, but there were too many of them. Finally, he was forced to turn and run into the forest with the hungry bees following him.

"We've got to get out of here," Deanna said to Derek.

"What about the moonstone?" Derek replied.

"Maybe we can come back with Iszarre," she answered.

"No," Derek said, surprising her. "If we leave, Eldrack will be free to search the orchard for the moonstone. By the time we return, he'll probably have it. We need to figure out where it is and get it while the bees are chasing him."

"So what do you suggest?" Deanna asked. "Where does the sun shine in all colors?"

"Well, I've been thinking," Derek began, "the only buildings we've seen in the Orchard are the planting sheds. Each one has a different color window. Maybe there's some sort of pattern. The windows might be the same color as the main type of fruit around the shed."

Tobungus ran up the small hill to their right and called out, "There's a whole bunch of sheds this way. It looks like an area with a lot of different types of fruit."

Derek and Deanna raced after Tobungus.

When they got to the sheds, they split up to see what they could find. After a few minutes, Derek was sure that he had found what they were looking for. "Deanna! Tobungus!" he shouted, "Get over here! I think I've found it."

They ran quickly over to Derek and saw him pointing to a stain-glassed window in the oldest, most run-down shed. "The sun would definitely shine in many colors as it passed through that. Just about every color is in that window," Derek said. They tried to open the door, but found that it was locked.

"Wait a second," Deanna said reaching into her pocket. She pulled out the key that the monkey had given her and inserted it into the lock. She struggled to turn the key, but finally heard a loud click, as the lock snapped open. Spurred on by excitement, they opened the door and searched the tables, old pots, bags of soil, and cabinets, but found nothing.

"Maybe we were wrong," Deanna said disappointedly. "We probably shouldn't stay in this shed too long, though. We don't know when Eldrack will return, and it looks like it's getting late in the afternoon," she added, pointing to the sunlight shining through the colorful window.

Tobungus stood staring at the window.

He tilted his head, trying to see something that had caught his attention. "Hey, Dino and Talon," he said.

"Well, at least you're getting closer with our names," Derek grinned in spite of himself.

"Sorry, maybe I should call you Ms. Wizard and Smart Mouth," Tobungus teased. "But seriously, look at the window. It looks like part of it is thicker than the rest." Pointing to the middle of the window, he added, "That green circle is sticking out."

Deanna climbed up on a rickety table and popped the second moonstone out of its hiding place. "Good eye, Tobungus," she said. She slipped the moonstone into her pocket, and they ran out of the shed where they were greeted by a chorus of odd, loud, irritating noises.

9 Bang a Gong

"What is that awful noise?" Deanna shouted, as she covered her ears.

"It's the peal of a gong," Tobungus yelled back. He pointed at a group of tall creatures holding giant metal gongs. "Eldrack has returned and brought the Gong Beaters of the Floddan Lowlands with him."

Derek and Deanna tried to run toward the orchard's exit. They had no idea where Eldrack was, but they had to escape the sickening ringing in their ears. They ran over a hill and turned down a path that led into a stand of trees. Even though they could no longer see the Gong Beaters, the sound of the gongs was so loud that it felt like it cut into their eardrums. They began to feel dizzy and nauseous. They had to escape before the Gong Beaters got any closer, but it was difficult to run because they had both hands clapped over their ears.

"This way," Tobungus yelled. He headed through a stand of tall trees and stopped in his tracks. Thirty feet in front of them stood Eldrack. He held up his hand and the gong beats softened.

"Give me the moonstone, and I will make the Gong Beaters stop," Eldrack hissed in a calm voice that magically cut through the noise of the gongs.

"Never," Deanna called. She pulled out the wand and began shouting every spell she could think of. Various fruits exploded, Eldrack's shirt turned olive green, and a Goma Bird sitting in a nearby tree turned into a walking potato. Derek stared at the potato, wondering what sort of spell Deanna had used.

Eldrack was surprised by Deanna's wild magical attack, but he soon came to his senses and used his wand to create a glowing shield in front of him. The rest of her spells simply bounced off of the shield harmlessly. "The moonstone!" he shouted. "Give it to me now." The gong beats grew deafening again.

Deanna was exhausted, but she would never give in to Eldrack. She grabbed Derek by the sleeve and pulled him back through the trees, hoping to find another exit from the orchard. The thick trees and rolling hills made it impossible to see the other sides of the orchard where an exit might be located. The pulsating gong tones continued to attack their ears.

Eldrack pulled out a baseball-sized glass

ball and threw it past Deanna and Derek. As the ball left his hand, it sucked him inside. When the ball landed, Eldrack reappeared in front of the frightened children.

Deanna pointed the Wand of Ondarell directly at Eldrack and yelled, "*Luminos vibratum.*" A beam of bright light shot from the wand and momentarily blinded the dark wizard. Deanna led the others back toward the entrance, realizing that it was the nearest way out. She didn't know how long Eldrack would be blinded, and she didn't wait around to find out.

Derek was out in front, looking frantically for anything that might help them. He saw Eldrack's glass ball flying overhead, and before the wizard could appear, he turned to his right and dove behind a large wooden structure that he thought was a planting shed. Deanna and Tobungus dove after him. When Derek looked up, he realized that they were hiding behind one of the massive bee hives. "Oh, no," was all he could say.

They could hear the giant bees buzzing through the hive's wooden walls. "Do something with that wand," Derek said.

Deanna remembered something called the Feather Spell from the Book of Spells. She opened the book quickly and found the magical words that she would need for the spell to work. She closed the book and began kicking the side of the hive.

"What are you doing?" Derek screamed. "These bees have stingers almost a foot long. We've made them crazy once today, why are you trying to make them come out?"

"Relax, Derek, I have an idea," she replied. "You and Tobungus need to be ready to grab my hands."

Deanna kept kicking the hive, and finally a few bees flew out. She immediately used her "*Explosio*" spell to blow up a few friddleberries on the far side of the friddleberry patch near the entrance to the orchard.

The bees sniffed the air and headed in the direction of the berries' fragrant juice. Their excited buzzing was loud, but it could not cover up the terrible gong tones. Deanna raised the wand and pointed it at the last bee. "*Feather light, transport until night*," she called out. A glowing purple and pink thread wrapped around the bee's legs and fluttered down to Deanna's hand.

She held her other hand out, and Derek grabbed it. With Tobungus holding Derek's other hand, they floated into the air, carried along by the bee. The spell had made them as light as a feather, and the bee did not even notice their extra weight.

When the bee approached the friddleberry vines, they hopped off and ran in the direction of the entrance. They still had a long way to run, but they were past Eldrack, so they thought they had a chance.

Derek looked back and saw Eldrack raise his arms. He seemed to be yelling into the trees on all sides. Seconds later, the sound of the gongs grew louder. Soon, the beat of the gongs was deafening as the gong beaters surrounded them in the trees. Derek and Deanna could barely walk because they had to keep their ears covered. The strange music felt like it was echoing inside their heads.

Eldrack raced toward them, sending a barrage of fiery spells into the vines around them. Deanna tried to raise her wand to use a spell, but as soon as she took her hands from her ears, a sharp pain shot through her. She quickly covered her ears again.

They stumbled on, but soon realized that they could not escape from Eldrack with the storm of gongs beating all around them. They now understood that the Gong Beaters did not just irritate people, they completely disabled them.

There was no way to use magic against Eldrack as long as the gongs were attacking their ear drums. The pain in their ears made them so dizzy that they couldn't walk in a straight line.

Tobungus tried to get Deanna's attention, but she was concentrating on stumbling forward. Finally, he ran and pushed Derek and Deanna to the ground. He pulled out his lemon from his bag, broke it in half, and began rubbing the juice on his ears. Then, he passed the lemon to Deanna and Derek and motioned that they should rub their ears with the lemon. As soon as their ears were covered, the sounds of the gongs faded.

"Now, Deanna," Tobungus said, "that should even things out a bit."

"Thanks, Tobungus," she said gratefully. She covered her ears and pretended that they were still hurting. She looked back and saw Eldrack closing in on them.

As Eldrack raised his wand for what was probably a final attack, he said, "Deanna, don't you think it's time to give up? You can't have much magic left."

She stared confidently at Eldrack and said, "I have enough." Her mind raced through all of the spells that she had read in the Book of Spells. Thinking back to what Derek had suggested about their battle with Green Thumb, Deanna quickly raised her wand and shouted, "*CYCLONICUS!*"

A cloud of dust and dirt began to spin around Eldrack and then he began to spin as well. He tried to fight the magical tornado, but he could not aim his wand accurately as he spun. Finally, he was sucked into the ground, just like the trees that Green Thumb had created in the Rhodian Flatlands.

"You were right, Derek," Deanna yelled. "That spell would have gotten rid of Green Thumb a lot faster."

"Let's get out of here before he comes back," Derek shouted back. They ran as fast as they could along the path toward the entrance that was now in sight.

Behind them, the ground rumbled violently. Derek looked back and saw Eldrack climbing out of a ragged hole in the ground.

Deanna sensed that Derek was slowing down. She looked back and saw Eldrack getting ready to toss his glass ball toward them. She shouted, "Come on, Derek! We can make it. The entrance is just ahead."

"No," Derek said. "He'll follow us out of the orchard. Leave it to me this time."

"What do you mean?" Deanna asked.

Derek didn't say anything. He had decided to use his own brand of magic, even if he could not get the hang of Elestra's yet. He picked up a thick branch lying next to the path and saw the glass ball flying through the air. He raced to catch up with it. Just before it hit the ground, he stopped and flipped his long blond hair out of his eyes. He swung the branch as hard as he could. He connected with the ball and sent it flying deep into the massive trees.

"Nice hit," Deanna called.

"Well my goal was to hit a homerun this summer," Derek replied. He loved baseball and had always been a great hitter, but he never hit a homerun in a real game. This one was better than any he could have hit on his team back home.

They turned back to the path and ran to the entrance. Just before they reached the edge of the orchard, a tall thin creature with four arms stepped out from behind a bush. He held a giant gong in two of his hands and two mallets in his other hands. He desperately tried to bang the gong loud enough to stop them.

Deanna saw a stand of slugfruit trees to

their left. She raised the wand toward the fruit and said, "*Levitato.*"

A huge slugfruit floated toward her. She made it hover in front of the Gong Beater who began to lick his lips. After a few seconds, he dropped the gong and chased the flying slugfruit up the path back into the orchard.

"I have an idea," Deanna said. She pointed the wand at the gong and said "*Levitato.*" The gong began to float. She flipped it upside down so that it looked like a shallow bowl. She then used the *Feather Spell* to make them as light as a feather again. They climbed onto the giant gong, and she used the wand to guide it out of the orchard.

10 River of the Dragon's Breath

Deanna looked to her right toward the Rhodian Flatlands and realized that if they went that way, they might have to battle Green Thumb again. A battle would slow them down and would give Eldrack time to catch up with them.

To her left, she saw a path that led further up Cauldron Mountain. She thought that they might be able to go up over the top of the mountain and down the other side. That direct route would also allow them to avoid the Forest of Confusion.

She guided the gong up the mountain path and watched as the rocky outcroppings grew closer. When they reached the summit, they saw a huge bubbling lake spreading out in all directions. There were small cone-shaped volcanoes rising out of the lake and sending clouds of steam into the air.

Beyond the lake, they could see cracks in the ground where orange lava crept to the surface. The heat from the lava gave the air an eerie orange glow.

Derek rubbed his eyes and looked past the lake a second time. "Is it my imagination or are there creatures in the lava over there?" he said, pointing to one of the bubbling pools.

"Those are volcarons," Tobungus said. "They're fire creatures. Those poor guys probably have to work in the Icelands. It looks like they're taking a vacation here." He pointed at a group of the strange creatures. "See, they're resting their aching feet in the lava."

Derek opened his mouth to say something, but he didn't know what to say about creatures lounging around a lava pit. Deanna just shook her head at the latest oddity of Elestra.

"I don't think we can get past this lake," Deanna said. "The gong can't stand up to those jets of steam. And I don't want to take the gong too high into the air because Eldrack would easily see us."

Suddenly, they heard the deep, pulsating banging of giant gongs. They looked back and saw that the Gong Beaters had left the orchard and were following them up the mountain. There was no route for them to take other than the one they were on. They could not go back the way they came.

Derek looked around. To the side of the

path, he saw the start of the River of the Dragon's Breath where the boiling waters left the volcanic lake. He watched as an area of the river bubbled and then exploded with a column of superheated steam.

The river was just as hot and steamy as the lake, but it also had rapids that ran over jagged volcanic rocks.

"I guess it's the river then," Derek said. Deanna and Tobungus looked confused. "We can use the gong to ride the rapids of the river. It will take us all the way down the mountain and back into Amemnop. Remember what we read, the River of the Dragon's Breath turns into the River of Tranquility?"

"Are you crazy?" Deanna asked. "That's the same river that sent geysers of steam at the goose. The goose barely avoided the geysers, and it was flying high above the river. We won't have any time to react if we're on the river. I don't see how we'll ever make it to the River of Tranquility."

"We won't have to worry about that." Pointing at the river, he said, "Watch how it happens."

They looked out over the river and saw another area bubbling. Within a few seconds, a jet of steam shot upward. "See what I mean? The river bubbles before a geyser shoots up."

"I don't know about this," Tobungus said. Before anyone could respond, they saw a group of Gong Beaters come closer into view down the path. "But, I guess we don't have any choice," he added.

They hopped off of the gong and pushed it to the river's edge. Deanna found a spell to keep the gong cool.

"Hey, Tuna," Tobungus said to Deanna, "Can you use that spell to freeze the river?"

"Deanna! It's Deanna," she said, exasperated at Tobungus' bungling of her name. "And, no, I can't freeze an entire volcanic river."

"Touchy, touchy," Tobungus said. "It was just a thought."

Derek picked up three large branches lying along the riverbank, so that they would each have something to use as an oar. The branches had black patches where lava had charred their edges, reminding them just how close they were to the mouth of the volcano.

Deanna pushed her branch against the ground to make sure that it was strong enough to hold up against the raging river. It creaked slightly, but it didn't break.

They all took deep breaths and climbed onto the gong. Derek used his branch to push them away from the shore. The water seemed thick, almost like slowly oozing lava running over flat land. The gong floated slowly at first, but it was quickly caught in the current. They picked up speed and bounced wildly as the gong entered a narrow part of the river where rapids tossed them from side to side.

They tried to use their branches to steer the gong around rocks that jutted out of the water and past bubbling areas where geysers would soon appear, but they continued to pick up speed and could not react quickly enough. To make matters worse, Tobungus dropped his branch into the river, when a small wave of hot water sloshed onto his arm.

Deanna looked back to see if he was alright and used the cooling spell to relieve the burn on his arm. With her attention on Tobungus, her branch hit a rock and broke in half.

The gong dropped over a steep rapid, and they had to grab hold of each other so they wouldn't fall out. They looked down the river in front of them and saw a huge group of rocks and volcanic glass rising out of the water.

"Deanna, do something with that wand," Derek yelled. "I can't steer this gong with one oar. These rapids are too wild."

Deanna pulled the wand out and tried to think of a spell that might help them. She was finding it hard to concentrate as they raced toward the rocks. They were seconds away from colliding with the rocks and being tossed into the boiling water of the river. Suddenly, the rocks exploded and the river flattened out. They floated along the smooth waters without any more problems.

"Wow!" Derek said, looking at Deanna. "What did you do?"

"I didn't do anything," Deanna said, looking around for some explanation of what had just happened. Up on a hill next to the river, she thought she saw a figure fading back into the trees. She couldn't tell if it was just one person because there was movement in the brush around the shadowy figure. "Did you see that?" she asked, pointing at the trees.

"See what?" Derek asked.

"I thought I saw someone up on the hill." She thought for a moment. "I know it sounds weird, but I think someone helped us past those rocks." She looked at Tobungus who was staring at the trees with a troubled look on his face. "What is it, Tobungus?"

"Nothing," he said, shaking his head. "I'm not sure what I saw. I mean, I saw something, but I don't know what it was."

"Well, I bet it was Iszarre," Derek said. "He was probably watching us all along. I knew he wouldn't let us go off on our own."

"We'll have to ask him," Deanna added. She wondered whether Glabber might have been there as well, since it seemed like there was more than one figure on the hill.

They reached the bottom of the mountain where the river was now filled with calm, cool water which flowed slowly toward Amemnop. They had obviously left the Baroka Valley because the trees were all normal sizes. They saw birds flying overhead that didn't look like passenger planes, and fish the size of school buses didn't jump over their gong boat.

They all settled in for the voyage down the river. "Tobungus," Derek said, "I've been wondering where you sleep here in Amemnop. We have a room at Glabber's, but I never asked what you do. Since we brought you here, I feel like we should be sure that you have someplace nice to stay."

"Oh, don't worry about me," Tobungus said. "I have friends everywhere. Besides, I can find a nice cool spot in the park and shrink back down into a pocket-sized toadstool, like when Aramaltus gave me to you. I have a clock that wakes me up, and then I can grow back to this size."

"That's pretty cool," Deanna said. "You know, we should remember that. You might be able to shrink down and not be noticed by Eldrack when we meet him sometime."

"I'm always up for an adventure," Tobungus said. "Though, I'm not sure that I like the idea of sitting out in the open as a tiny mushroom with Eldrack walking around. He'd probably step on me on purpose. I'd still be faster than him, though," he added laughing.

They all got a good laugh out of the idea of a tiny mushroom whirling around with the caped dark wizard trying to step on him.

The river was so smooth that they were able to lay back in the gong and watch the clouds pass overhead for a while. They realized how tired they were after such a long day. Tobungus started snoring almost instantly, while Derek and Deanna struggled to stay awake, thinking about what they would learn from the vision of

Mindoro hiding the second moonstone.

After a long relaxing gong ride, they sat up and saw the buildings in Amemnop rising along the horizon. At first, just the tallest towers of the Library, the Tower of the Moons, and the Magian Magical Research Academy were visible. As they neared the city, more buildings came into view.

At the edge of town, along the river, they passed the zoo and bestiary. "I bet they have some bizarre animals in there," Deanna said.

"It always depends on the types of deals they can make," Tobungus said.

"What do you mean?" Deanna asked.

"You have to remember that most creatures in Elestra can talk and have their own societies, so the people who run the zoo can't capture them and put them in a zoo like they do in your world," Tobungus explained. "The people who run the zoo pay the creatures to live there and to tell visitors about themselves."

"Another typically strange Elestran place," Derek said.

"You may think so," Tobungus said, "but it might be useful for you two to go there and meet creatures from the places you will be exploring. You might find a lot of information that can help you on your journeys."

"I hadn't thought of it like that," Derek said. Deanna agreed that a visit to the zoo could be an important learning experience.

Twenty minutes later, they were safely back on dry land in the City of Light. Derek used his branch to steer them to a wooden pier where dozens of small boats were tied up. They climbed onto the pier and walked through town to the Tower of the Moons.

The Second Vision

Evening was upon them and the moons were low in the eastern sky. Deanna pulled the moonstone out of her pocket and looked through it at the second moon. A gust of warm wind rushed over her and she felt the magic course through her body.

She handed the moonstone to Derek who looked at the moon through it. He felt the same sensation, a warm, tingly wind that passed right through him, and he handed the moonstone back to her.

They entered the Tower of the Moons and climbed the steep spiral staircase that wrapped around the inside of the tower's walls. When they reached the top, Deanna placed the moonstone in the second slot on the bronze strip that arched over the tower's highest room. There were now two moonstones in the arch, but there were still thirteen open slots.

"You know," Derek began, "Eldrack's going to be more determined to stop us now that we have two moonstones."

"We'll deal with him when the time comes," Deanna said bravely. "But now, it's time to see the second moonstone's vision." Iszarre had told them that when they put a moonstone in the arch, they could look though it at that stone's moon and see a vision of the time when the moonstone was last held by its Guardian.

Deanna and Derek put their heads together and peered through the shimmering green stone. They felt like they were inside the vision, watching what was happening, as if they were right there. They saw a dark scene. It seemed to be night time, and there were clouds swirling around them. They were moving, soaring through the thick mist. Below, they saw what appeared to be a river. They realized that it was the same river that they had ridden down earlier in the day. The mist was the steam rising from the boiling waters.

They soared onward and shot out of the clouds toward the Atteelian Orchard. It was still dark in their vision, and there were flashes of lightning. They stopped and looked around. They felt the wind whipping through their hair. A storm was brewing. An eerie orange light lit the top of the mountain to their right.

In front of them, darkness was cut by the

nearly constant flashes in the sky. They squinted, trying to see through the growing storm. From behind the planting sheds, came a man they had seen once before, frozen in a tube in the Cave of Imprisonment. It was Mindoro, the second Mystical Guardian. He wore the flowing purple and green robes that a great wizard would wear. His wand was raised, and he looked frantic.

They turned to see what could have frightened such a powerful wizard. They saw Eldrack walking up the path, his long black cape lifted by the wind. There were waves of Noctorns flying behind him, as well as other creatures they did not recognize—birds with beaks that looked like knife blades and animals with the body of a cougar and the head of a fanged lizard. They saw an army of Gong Beaters, but luckily they couldn't hear their terrible song in the vision.

They turned back to Mindoro who was firing spells toward Eldrack and his army. Walls of stone appeared on the path where Mindoro aimed. The Noctorns circled around Mindoro's back, so he turned and created another wall. Soon, there were walls on all sides of him. He seemed protected and captured at the same time.

Eldrack just stood and watched Mindoro

trying desperately to save himself. He made no move to attack, letting the Mystical Guardian tire himself out.

Eldrack pulled out a tiny orange glass bead and held it in his hand. He raised his wand toward the sky and muttered a few words which they could not hear. The clouds above Mindoro began to spin faster and faster. A cone that looked like a slow-moving tornado began to drop from the clouds. When the cone was nearly down to Mindoro, Eldrack flipped the glass bead into the swirling storm. The magical tornado nearly reached the ground. Its tiny funnel cloud fingers grabbed at Mindoro's robe. Orange light wrapped around Mindoro, and he suddenly disappeared in a flash that looked like a flame torn apart by the wind. Eldrack flicked his wand quickly and sent a wave of flickering light at the stone walls which collapsed under the massive magical attack.

Eldrack waved his hands at the clouds and waited a few moments as the storm died down. Then, he walked to the stone pile and climbed to its center. His next move surprised the twins more than anything else they had seen in the vision. Eldrack simply vanished.

Derek and Deanna blinked several times

and returned from their vision. Their hair was messed up, as if they had been standing in the storm in the Atteelian Orchard that they had just seen. They thought that this vision seemed more real than the first, like they felt more of it. Their skin tingled like they had just come inside on a windy day.

Silently, each thinking about the vision, they left the Tower of the Moons and headed back to Glabber's Grub Hut. Something about the vision didn't seem right, but neither of them could decide what that was.

When they arrived, Iszarre was standing behind the counter with the snake wizard Glabber, talking to Tobungus who was eating a bowl of green, vibrating cereal. "You must be hungry," Iszarre called out.

"I'm starved," Derek replied. He was still confused about the vision, but decided to talk to Deanna about it later. They sat at the counter, ready to eat a huge meal.

"What do you like on your pizza?" Iszarre asked.

"Lots of cheese," Deanna said.

"I like mush..." Derek began, but stopped and looked nervously at Tobungus.

"You're a barbarian!" Tobungus yelled,

pretending to be deeply offended. Then, he laughed, "The little mushrooms you eat on your pizza are really just mushrooms, so there's no problem."

Iszarre brought over three pizzas and a bowl of fruit. "I think we've had enough fruit for one day," Deanna joked.

They ate most of their pizza before sitting back to tell Iszarre about their adventure in the Baroka Valley. He smiled widely, clearly pleased that they had beaten Eldrack to another moonstone.

When they described their vision and how they felt like they were a part of the scene that they had witnessed, Iszarre said, "My, my, your power has grown more quickly than I expected. You shouldn't be able to connect with the magic that holds these visions this easily yet. I'll have to give this some thought."

"There was something different about this vision," Derek said. Iszarre looked at him curiously.

"This vision was more real," Deanna said. Iszarre turned toward her and nodded that he understood what she meant.

"It's not just that," Derek said. "I thought we were supposed to see the last moments when the Guardian hid the moonstone. We never saw Mindoro holding the moonstone. He was in the Atteelian Orchard where we found the moonstone, but it seemed like the vision showed us a time after he had hidden it."

Iszarre thought for a few moments. "As I told you, your ability to see the visions will grow along with your other magical powers. It is possible that you saw a small part of a larger vision—perhaps the end of the vision, after Mindoro had hidden the moonstone."

"That's probably it," Deanna said. "After all, we did see Mindoro very near the planting shed where we found the moonstone. He may have hidden the moonstone and run out to find Eldrack ready to ambush him."

"But, why didn't Eldrack search for the stone?" Derek asked. "He used that storm to capture Mindoro, but then, instead of staying in the Orchard to search for the stone, he just disappeared."

"It is possible that the storm opened an entrance to the Cave of Imprisonment," Iszarre mused.

"I hadn't thought of that," Deanna replied.

"Eldrack may have followed Mindoro to the Cave to make sure that he was captured or to make him reveal where he had hidden the moonstone," Iszarre said, stroking his long beard.

As they listened to Iszarre, Deanna remembered the figure on the ridge who had saved them during their river ride. "By the way, thanks for helping us on the river," she said.

"What do you mean?" Iszarre replied curiously.

"We were about to smash into these huge rocks in the river, and we didn't know what to do. Someone used magic to destroy the rocks and help us float to the safe part of the river. We figured it was you." Deanna said.

At that moment, Tobungus dropped his spoon and bent over to pick it up. When he straightened up, he stood and walked over to put the spoon in a bin of dirty dishes. Derek watched him, wondering why he suddenly seemed so nervous.

"I was here the whole time. Well, I should say I was here the whole time after returning from my meeting with King Barado," Iszarre replied thoughtfully, looking over at Tobungus. "It appears we have another mystery to figure out."

"How was your meeting with the king?" Tobungus asked, as he returned to the table, clearly wanting to change the subject.

"It was very pleasant to go to the castle again," Iszarre said. "King Barado is very pleased with your success against Eldrack so far. He is eager to hear more good news."

"Well, we still have a long way to go," Deanna said.

"Yes, but you are proving to be powerful and clever," Iszarre replied. "It's nice to have magical power, but it's even better to know how to use it in ways that your opponents won't expect."

"I suppose you're right," Deanna said. "Derek has come up with really great strategies against Eldrack. I don't think he's expected some of the things that we've done."

"I don't think Eldrack has expected you to be able to use the wand as well as you have either," Derek added.

"Exactly," Iszarre said. "You both just have to keep it up. Always work together and you will be the wizards who finally defeat the most evil wizard that Elestra has ever seen." Looking at their empty cups, he said, "Oh, my, I'll go fill those up."

"I bet it was Dad," Derek whispered to Deanna when Iszarre left to refill their drinks. "I bet he ignored Iszarre's warning." At the end of their last journey, Iszarre had told them that he would write to their father and tell him that they were safe and that he should stay out of Elestra because Eldrack would be able to sense his power and try to capture him.

"Well, if it was Dad, I hope he stays hidden," Deanna said. "If we can increase our power and join him, that would really help against Eldrack."

She looked over toward the counter and saw Iszarre staring at her, as if he had overhead what she said. His look was completely unreadable, and she didn't want to ask him if she was right.

Through the diner's windows, Derek and Deanna could see that the last rays of sunlight had disappeared, and Elestra's fifteen moons bathed Amemnop in a sea of soft light. Deanna yawned and fought to stay awake.

"Perhaps you should head to bed," Iszarre said, returning with a final glass of water for each of them to take to their room.

Reluctantly, she nodded and rose from the counter. Derek patted Tobungus' hand and said "Good night" to Iszarre and Glabber.

As Deanna and Derek walked toward the

stairs, Iszarre added softly, "With a full night to sleep, you may dream about the Desert of the Crescent Dunes."

"Sounds hot," Derek replied grinning sleepily at Deanna. "We'd better wear shorts."

Turn the page. The adventure continues…

Epilogue

Derek and Deanna have now found the first two moonstones and defeated Eldrack in Amemnop and in the Atteelian Orchard, but there is much more to do and much more to learn.

In their bits of free time, Deanna and Derek continued to wander through the State Library of Magia to find out more about the places, people, and creatures they have encountered. The following pages will tell you what they learned, and perhaps, just as importantly, what they didn't learn.

Eldrack's Minions

Derek and Deanna sat at a table in the Library and tried to decide what they should look up in the magical books. "You know," Derek said, "we weren't able to find anything about Eldrack last time, and he is the one we really need to learn about. If we can't find out about Eldrack, how about looking up the creatures who follow him?"

"That's a great idea," Deanna said. "If any of those things we've already seen show up again, we would be able to use the information to plan a strategy during future battles."

"Right, and maybe we can get an idea about why they are helping him," Derek added.

"Okay, so we need to get books that talk about the Gong Beaters and Green Thumb," Deanna said.

"Don't forget the Noctorns that we faced when we found the first moonstone," Derek said.

"Good point!" Deanna said. "I'll tell the librarian." She got up and walked over to the tiny fairy librarian's desk.

"May I help you?" the six inch tall librarian said, flapping the shimmering wings on her back.

"Yes, we need books that discuss the Noctorns, the Gong Beaters of the Floddan Lowlands, and the forest elf called Green Thumb," Deanna said.

"Can you tell me where Green Thumb lives?" the librarian asked.

"I think he lives in the Baroka Valley," Deanna answered. "That's where we faced him."

"Hmm, let's see," the librarian muttered. "I think we should try it like this." She turned toward the shelves and said, "Show me books about Noctorns, the Gong Beaters of the Floddan Lowlands, and Forest Elves of the Baroka Valley who oppose King Barado."

A shimmering mist seemed to float up toward the shelves and the titles of books began to light up. "Book fairies," the librarian called out, "retrieve the books."

A wave of tiny book fairies rushed out from under the desk and pulled the books off of the shelves. Within a minute a stack of ten or twelve books sat on the table in front of Derek.

Deanna pulled a chair next to Derek's and waved the Wand of Ondarell over the stack of books and said, *"Explanatum."* The stack shuddered, telling Deanna that the books were ready to give them the information they wanted.

"Okay," Deanna said to the first book, "Can you tell me anything about the Noctorns?"

The book opened, almost like it was bored. A tired voice said:

> *Noctorns are flying creatures which combine human-like arms and legs, the head of a coyote, and wings that allow them to fly. Noctorns can grow to seven feet tall, with a wing span of eight feet.*
>
> *Noctorns are allergic to light, and only come out of their dens at night. Sunlight can cause serious injury to them, and artificial light will knock them off of their feet. Even candlelight will make them sneeze.*
>
> *Even though Noctorns look ferocious, they are famous for their gentle nature and their fascination with cheese. They are native to the Mundallon Valley where they hold seasonal cheese festivals which draw crowds from all over Elestra.*
>
> *Their festivals include art and music from all regions of Elestra, but it is their*

own music which has caused a great deal of trouble in recent years. Modern Noctorn music has been described as an argument between a harmonica and a howling dog.

King Barado was a special guest at the Noctorn Summer Festival three hundred and one years ago and condemned the music that he claimed gave him a headache the size of a Barokan Rattlefish

The Noctorns tend to be very sensitive and were highly insulted by the king's comments. They temporarily cancelled their festivals and issued a statement of protest against the king's musical tastes.

King Barado promised to review their request for an apology, but he has continuously avoided it.

The Noctorns have broken diplomatic relations with Barado's court, and some witnesses claim to have seen groups of Noctorns working for a dark wizard.

It is not known if those Noctorns are working alone or if they are part of an official opposition to the king.

The book closed its cover and sighed, as if it was glad to stop talking about the Noctorns.

"Well," Deanna said, a bit surprised, "it seems that the Noctorns joined Eldrack because they were mad at King Barado."

"Yeah, but it sounds a little crazy to join Eldrack over an insult about your music," Derek added.

"Let's see what we can find out about the Gong Beaters," Deanna said. Turning to the stack of books, she said, "Can any of you tell us about the Gong Beaters of the Floddan Lowlands?"

A book in the middle of the stack made a sound like a hiccup and squeezed out of the stack and settled onto the table in front of Deanna. It opened its cover and carefully flipped the pages until it found what it was looking for. A voice that was tinged with hints of a British accent said:

> The Gong Beaters come from the Floddan Lowlands which is an area on the border between Magia and the Icelands. The Lowlands are marshy and cool.
>
> The Gong Beaters are a group of Floddans who migrated to the Lowland area after being kicked out of the city of Floddu Prime. This city is the site of the

Magian Academy of Music which is one of the top three music schools in Elestra.

Floddan children study music extensively and most join bands or orchestras before they become teenagers. The high point of the Floddan musical year is the Annual Slugfruit Parade through the streets of Floddu Prime.

Nearly three hundred and twenty years ago, a group of Floddans tried to create a new symphony played only on gongs. The group was banned from performing in the parade because the sound was so painful to listeners.

This group of Gong Beaters felt humiliated and left the city to find a new place to practice and perform their style of music. They settled in the Lowlands where no other Floddans lived and have developed a separate Floddan society since that time.

The Gong Beaters tried for years to develop a pleasing gong concerto and asked if they could play it for King Barado. They believed that if the king liked their music, the rest of the Floddans would want them to come back to their home city and play in the parade.

When he heard the gong music, King Barado grabbed his ears and screamed in pain. The Gong Beaters stormed out and accused the king of favoring the other Floddans over them.

In the years since, the Gong Beaters of the Floddan Lowlands have been allied to forces opposed to King Barado.

"That's the second group that joined Eldrack over a musical argument," Deanna said.

"Hmm," Derek said. "I wonder if Eldrack is finding groups that are mad at King Barado about something and then tricking them into joining him."

"That could be," Deanna replied. "The Noctorns and Gong Beaters don't sound like evil creatures. It just sounds like they were mad at the king. I can't see that being the reason that Green Thumb is working with Eldrack, though."

"Yes," Derek said slowly. "But, remember that Green Thumb did that 'I'm so great' song and dance. That's enough to make anyone sick."

"That's true," Deanna said. "Let's see what we can find out about Green Thumb from the books." She asked the pile of books which of them could tell them about Green Thumb.

Two of the books popped out of the stack at the same time and started to have a slap fight with their covers. Deanna separated them and asked the one who seemed to be losing to tell them what it knew.

The cover opened slowly, as if it was sore from the fight. The book said, "Ow!" as it opened, and then a nervous voice said:

> *Green Thumb is a Forest Elf from the Baroka Valley. He studied to become an orchard master in one of the Baroka Valley's many orchards, but was fired so that another elf named Doterius could become the master of the Glafeerian Orchard.*
>
> *Green Thumb claimed that he was the best grower among Forest Elves and left the orchards to practice his magic in the Rhodian Flatlands.*

The book's cover closed with a groan. The other book was twitching and making a growling sound toward it.

Deanna aimed the wand at the second book and said, "You be good!" The book instantly became quiet. She thanked the first book and turned to the second book. "Okay, if you can be nice, you can tell us what you know about Green Thumb."

The book hopped into place in front of her and threw its cover open. A panting voice said:

> *Green Thumb became angrier over the years after he was fired. He developed new spells and was able to conjure trees from the bare ground in seconds.*
>
> *He went to every orchard in the Baroka Valley but none of them would give him a job. He finally became so angry that he joined Eldrack."*

The book closed its cover quickly and let out a shaky, "Oops!"

The books on the towering shelves began to shudder and gasp. Wind swirled through the library and picked up the book.

"No," the book said. "It was a mistake." The wind carried the book up to the highest shelf where only one other book sat.

As the wind died down, Deanna looked over to the fairy librarian. "What was that all about," Deanna asked.

"There are rules for the books," the

librarian explained. "Some rules are hidden, and we only learn about them if a book breaks them. That book said something it should not have said, so it was taken to the Shelf of Isolation."

"What did it say?" Deanna asked.

"It mentioned Eldrack," Derek replied. "None of the other books have spoken his name while we have been trying to find out about him."

"Yeah, but didn't a book mention him when we were finding out about the fountain?" Deanna asked.

The librarian flew over and said, "It may be that the books are under a spell that prohibits them from answering certain questions about Eldrack and his activities. They may be permitted to mention Eldrack in some cases, especially in cases where the information about Eldrack is well known."

"But I thought everything about Eldrack was deleted from the books," Deanna said.

"True," the librarian said mysteriously. "But, you will find that the books have a long memory. Just because something is deleted does not mean that the books will forget it."

"But who makes the rules for the books?" Derek wondered aloud.

"Who indeed," the librarian replied.

The Wand of Ondarell

The book fairies swooped down and took the teetering stack of books back to their shelves. Deanna and Derek sat at the table, wondering if they could trust the books if they couldn't tell them everything about their enemies.

The fairy librarian sensed their concern and said, "Don't worry too much about the books. They will tell you almost anything you want to know, and if they are being stopped by a magical spell, you will be able to tell that. You saw how the books shuddered and became nervous. They will do that any time they are afraid of the information you request."

"That's good to know," Deanna said. The librarian fluttered back to her desk, leaving the twins to discuss their next search.

"Magic seems to control this library," Derek said, with a smile hinting at a new book request.

"You're right about that," Deanna said. "So, how do we ask the books for information about magic when most of the books here contain some information about magic?" She sat staring at the wand that she held in her hands.

"Brilliant," Derek said, following Deanna's gaze. He jumped up and ran over to the librarian's desk. Deanna watched him, wondering what he meant. "We'd like to see books that discuss the Wand of Ondarell," Derek said to the librarian.

She looked over her glasses at him and gave him a sly smile. "You're very clever," she said. She turned to the shelves and said, "Show me the book that talks about the Wand of Ondarell and other related wands."

Derek looked at the shelves but didn't see any of the titles lighting up. The librarian was staring almost straight up toward the ceiling. "I'll be right back with your book," she said. She zipped up and out of sight. A few seconds later, she swooped back down, towing a tattered, old book.

Derek followed her to the table and thanked her for her help.

Deanna tapped the cover of the book and said, "*Explanatum*." She turned to Derek with a nod.

"Please tell us what you know about the Wand of Ondarell," Derek said to the book.

Nothing happened for several seconds. Finally, the cover opened slowly. A soft, ancient voice, somewhere just above a whisper began:

The Wand of Ondarell is a member of a special class of wands known as channeling wands. These wands can only be used by the most powerful wizards because they connect to advanced streams of magic that flow through the wizards.

Channeling wands act like a magnifying lens and focus the strong magic in the wizard to create powerful spells. Normal wizards do not have enough magic to control these wands, and they often find that their spells fire back at them.

Channeling wands are extremely rare. Channeling wands are made by wandsmiths who gather the wood of the Partempus Tree and soak it deep in one of the magical wells for one hundred years.

After the period of soaking, the wand is placed in a pot that contains sand from the deepest point in the Ocean of Eternity. The pot is slowly roasted in the Flame of Seven Colors to harden the wand. Finally, the wand is taken to the pit of the Kutama Volcano where it takes its final shape.

Only four channeling wands are currently known to exist. The Wand of Ondarell and its twin, the Wand of Kutama, as well as the Wand of Liadorra, were all created from the same branch of the Partempus Tree.

The other channeling wand is held by the great wizard Iszarre who oversaw the creation of his wand personally.

Other channeling wands have been made over the centuries. Some have been lost and some have been destroyed in magical battles. There are rumors of other channeling wands existing, but no one has been able to confirm these rumors.

The book stopped talking, but its cover stayed open, almost as if it knew that there would be more questions.

Deanna looked at Derek and then back to the book. She thought for a moment and then said, "You have explained that the Wand of Ondarell is one of three wands that were created together. If these other wands still exist, where are they?" She was thinking that if they could get another wand, Derek could use one, and they would be much more powerful.

The book continued telling them about the wands:

> *The Wand of Ondarell and the two other wands were separated from each other hundreds of years ago. The Wand of Liadorra is sealed in a chamber in King Barado's castle.*
>
> *The Wand of Kutama was stolen by a dark wizard in the distant past. There is no other information on this wand.*

Once the book was quiet again, Derek said, "Hey, Deanna, maybe we can find out who makes those wands and get another one."

"Another wand would be good, but the book said that it takes over a hundred years to make one," Deanna said. "Although, maybe the person who makes them already has one ready."

The book heard Deanna's comments and interrupted:

> *The Partempus Tree is located in the Bagayama Mountains. The wandsmiths who have made all of the channeling*

wands are from the Betarolio family living in the Baroka Valley.

The family maintains a partnership with the creatures who are able to descend into the Magical Wells to place the wood and retrieve it later. Most beings cannot survive in the deepest parts of the Wells near the Ruby Core.

There is no further information on the Betarolio family or wands that they are currently making.

The book closed its cover, telling Deanna and Derek that there was no other information about the Wand of Ondarell or its sister wands.

Deanna signaled for the librarian to take the book back to its resting place. Turning to Derek, she said, "I'd like to find out more about the Betarolio family, but I'm really hungry. Maybe we can look them up next time."

"Yeah, sure," Derek said, looking toward the ceiling. Without looking away, he said, "I'd like to know what's in that other book on the Shelf of Isolation."

"That would be interesting," Deanna said. "Let's ask Iszarre if he knows anything about the shelf first. I don't want to get in trouble for asking about the book."

"Good point," Derek added. "Let's head to Glabber's for lunch.

Preview of Book 3

Derek and Deanna seek the third moonstone in *The Desert of the Crescent Dunes*. Derek visits the mysterious Gula Badu to read a prophecy that hints at an unthinkable alliance. The twins travel outside of Magia to the Desert Realm and meet a girl named Dahlia who feeds them sugary lizard tails and reads carpets.

Of course, Tobungus is miserable in the dry heat of the desert, but their new travel partner Zorell, the cat who seems to hate Tobungus, basks in the hot sun as well as in the shadows of giant cat statues.

They have to pick the right archway to enter, or they will find themselves wandering an underground labyrinth for years. Sightless snakes that spring into the air, colossal knifebirds, tentacled sand beasts, and Eldrack himself stand in their way. Floating over the Great Snort Pit may be the only escape.

The first chapter begins on the next page, and the story ends in the pages of *The Desert of the Crescent Dunes*.

1 Here, Kitty, Kitty!

"*Derek. . . Derek,*" an old, soft voice whispered. Derek Hughes stirred from a restful sleep to see who was calling him. "*Derek.*" The voice sounded so old that he imagined the words struggling through a layer of dust.

"Who's there?" Derek asked nervously.

"*Derek,*" the voice sounded tired. "*The library. . . the ancient archives. . . prophecy.*"

Derek rubbed his sleepy eyes and mumbled, "the library?"

"*The ancient archives.*" The voice trailed off as it whispered, "*Gula Badu.*"

"What?" Derek shot back. There was no reply. "What's Gula Badu?"

Silence filled the room. Derek looked around in the darkness, trying to see any movement. After several minutes, he realized that there was no one else in the room other than his twin sister Deanna. He got out of bed and walked across to the big cushy chair by the window. He spent the last hour before the sun rose trying to figure out what the voice was telling him.

He thought back to the night when he and Deanna had seen their grandfather disappear into the old lantern in their backyard and learned about the magical adventures that awaited them in this strange land of Elestra. It was on that night that their grandfather told them that they were the last of the Mystical Guardians. They were Elestra's only hope to recover the lost moonstones, powerful magical jewels which would enable them to defeat the evil wizard Eldrack.

It still seemed like a dream. It had been exciting, but he missed his parents, even though the great wizard Iszarre explained that his father must stay out of Elestra to remain safe.

Iszarre had arranged for them to stay in a room upstairs at Glabber's Grub Hut. He had even placed a magical spell on the room to make it look exactly like the room the twins shared back home. Derek could hear Glabber clanging pots and dishes in the kitchen below and hoped that the sounds from the diner would wake Deanna.

But it wasn't until the morning had replaced the long, dark night that Deanna stirred in her soft bed, instinctively hiding from the sun's rays beneath the billowing white blankets that covered her like a sky full of clouds.

"Come on, Deanna," Derek called. "Get up. We've got a lot to do today."

"Hold on," Deanna replied groggily. "I'm trying to get used to the light."

"Deanna," Derek said, "It's cloudy today. Get out of bed so we can get to the library."

Derek and Deanna had to go to the library to learn about the Desert of the Crescent Dunes. Iszarre had hinted that this was the location of the next moonstone. For the first time, they would be leaving Magia, so they wanted to gather as much information as possible. Derek also wanted to find out if the voice that had awakened him was leading him to something important.

Deanna finally pushed back the covers and slowly climbed out of bed. As Derek waited impatiently for Deanna to gather her clothes, he looked out the window toward a park they had seen on their walks back to Glabber's Grub Hut from the Tower of the Moons.

Each of the park's entrances had a small fountain with a statue of one of Elestra's great wizards from the past. They had hoped to spend some time in the park to learn more about Elestra's history, but for now, they had to focus on gathering the moonstones before the dark wizard Eldrack got to them.

As Derek stood deep in thought, looking at the fountain, he saw something that he couldn't quite explain. "Huh?" he mumbled, as he started to piece together what was happening.

Deanna looked over and saw Derek's look of surprise. "What's wrong, Derek?" she asked.

"I'll be right back," Derek answered as he grabbed the Wand of Ondarell and ran out the door. He flew down the stairs and out into the street toward the fountain. There, he saw his friend Tobungus, the mushroom man, setting a plate next to the fountain's outer stone wall. A foot-long fish rested on the plate. Tobungus could barely hold back his laughter as he put his devious plan into motion.

Off to the right, Zorell, the talking cat, was crouching and ready to pounce on the fishy feast. He was so desperate to get to the fish that he didn't stop to think how odd Tobungus' actions were.

To the left, hidden by bushes, two large, extremely hungry looking saber-tooth dogs crouched, drooling and ready to pounce once Zorell made his move.

"Out of the way, Tobungus," Derek shouted as he raised the wand.

Tobungus was already on his way to a hiding place where he could watch Zorell walk into his trap. He didn't seem to hear Derek's command. But, he definitely noticed what happened next.

"*Gigantum pisce*," Derek yelled as the fanged beasts leapt from behind the bushes. A flash of blue light hit the fish and it began to swell. Its tail inflated first, followed by the rest of its body. Soon, the gray fish was nearly fifteen feet long and looked like a small blimp.

Derek rarely used the wand, partly because Deanna was so skilled with it, and partly because he was not very confident in his magical abilities. He smiled to himself, thinking that he had finally made a spell work exactly as he wanted it to.

The hungry saber-toothed dogs tripped over one another as they backed away from the giant mutant fish. They turned quickly and fled, knocking several people to the ground along the cobblestone street. Zorell ran to Derek's side which made Derek feel more confident in his use of the wand.

"No! Wait! Come back," Tobungus shouted. He quickly fell silent, however, when he turned to see Derek staring and Zorell glaring at him. "What?" He asked a little too innocently. Zorell hissed and prepared to pounce.

"Alright, you two," Derek said, moving to stand between Tobungus and Zorell. "Let's go get some breakfast and talk this over."

"Aren't you going to do something with the fish?" Zorell asked.

Derek turned around and saw a growing number of people in the park stopping and staring in amazement at the massive fish. "Actually, I don't know the counterspell," he whispered, as they hurried back to Glabber's Grub Hut.

Along the way, Derek had to walk between his two friends. Zorell had his claws out. Tobungus had a squirt bottle filled with a brown liquid that smelled like burned pickles and wet dog aimed at Zorell.

Tobungus had been given to the twins by the Wood Frog Aramaltus as their first adventure started. Zorell joined them later after helping them battle a rogue fairy at the library. They were both helpful to the twins, but they seemed to hate each other. Sometimes their arguing was humorous, and sometimes it was distracting.

Just when the cat seemed ready to pounce, Derek said, "settle down, Zorell."

"Zorell?" Tobungus said. "Did he tell you his name was Zorell?"

"My name is Zorell," the cat hissed back.

"That's funny," Tobungus replied rubbing a finger across his spongy chin, "I spent the past four months thinking your name was NibbleBits." He raised his squirt bottle, expecting Zorell to lash out with his dagger-like claws.

Zorell took a deep breath and turned to Derek. "Do you see what I have had to put up with? The family I traveled with had a little girl who called me a lot of silly names, but my name is Zorell."

"Of course it is, precious widdle NibbleBits," Tobungus said.

"Tobungus," Derek warned, "that's enough. The next time I see you two fighting, I'm going straight to Iszarre."

The threat of the great wizard's disapproval was like a powerful magical spell. Tobungus and Zorell remained quiet as they entered the diner and found an open table for breakfast. Derek was happy to have them silent, while he watched the snake wizard Glabber place a stack of friddleberry pancakes in front of him.

When he was about to take his first bite of the pancakes, Deanna came down the worn wooden stairs and sat down in front of what she thought was her own food.

She looked down at a bowl of wiggling worms and orange leaves and jumped back in surprise. "Glabber," she shouted, "what *is* this?"

The sleek serpent wizard glided across the floor and rose up to the table. "Oops, sorry my dear," he hissed, "that was meant for my brother who is visiting from the Desert Realm."

"Your brother's here?" Derek asked, looking toward the large window behind the counter.

"Oh, yes," Glabber answered. "He's in the kitchen chasing his breakfast." As if on cue, a loud crash from breaking glasses came from the kitchen. "I'll be right back," Glabber said. "Oh, and I'll get you something a bit more to your liking." He grabbed the bowl and slithered away to get Deanna a plate of pancakes.

"It sounds like Glabber's brother is another Tobungus," Derek joked.

"Hmm?" Deanna said, a bit distracted. She was still grossed out from seeing the bowl of worms, and she was wondering where Derek had gone with the wand so quickly.

Before Deanna could ask Derek why he had run out of the room, Iszarre walked in through the diner's main door. Instead of his usual apron, the old wizard was wearing overalls and grimy boots. He was covered in dirt, and didn't look too happy.

"What happened to you?" Deanna asked.

"The magical armies are stirring," Iszarre said, sitting on a chair by the counter.

He flicked his wand toward the window to the kitchen, and a large mug of purple liquid floated to him. He took a long drink and sat back to relax. He offered no further explanation of his cryptic statement.

Derek and Deanna simply looked at each other.

Glabber, the snake wizard, returned to their table and set a plate of pancakes in front of Deanna. He explained, "Every five hundred years, the seventeen magical armies rise from the underground catacombs. The armies join powerful wizards to decide who controls Elestra. The Army of the Ruby Dawn always follows the leaders of Magia, and Iszarre wanted to be sure that they are able to come to the surface. He's been digging near the old entrance to the catacombs since last night."

"Why wouldn't they have been able to come to the surface?" Derek asked.

"Iszarre heard a rumor that Eldrack was trying to put a spell over the catacombs' entrance to keep it closed," Glabber explained.

"A rumor?" Derek said.

"A prophecy, actually." Iszarre said. He hobbled over and sank into a chair next to Deanna. He picked up a pancake and mopped his sweaty forehead with it. Looking at the soaked pancake, he said, "I'll get this back to you after I clean it."

"No," Deanna said quickly, "you can keep it."

Iszarre looked surprised and thanked Deanna for the gift. He took another drink of the purple liquid and began to explain about the magical armies.

"Sometimes the armies follow the first powerful wizard who comes along," he said, "instead of waiting to see who the rightful leaders of each kingdom are. It is important to find the armies quickly so that they join us against Eldrack."

"Are you saying that there will be a war in Elestra?" Deanna asked nervously.

"Oh, no. It's not quite like that," Iszarre began. "It's more like a magical tournament. The armies battle each other with magical spells. When warriors are hit by spells, they simply return to the catacombs until the next battle. When one army wins the magical tournament, though, that army gives all of its magic to the wizard leading it. If Eldrack gets an army to follow him and they win, he will become even more powerful."

"I guess we better make sure that he doesn't win, then," Derek said grimly.

"But how does a wizard get a magical army to follow him?" Deanna asked.

"Some of the magical armies always follow the strongest wizards or paramages from one of the Six Kingdoms," Iszarre said. "Other armies are less predictable. You'll find that music is a powerful force in Elestra. Some armies are drawn to magical music. Eldrack may trick them into believing that he controls the source of music that they follow."

"So, if we find all of the moonstones and start all of the magical instruments, will that help us keep the armies on our side?" Derek asked.

"Oh, you will find that the music that will play after you return all of the moonstones to the arch will influence the armies," Iszarre said. "But, it will also help you in ways you cannot even imagine yet," he added with the smallest smile creasing his face. "But for now, you have another moonstone to find. If I recall correctly, you'll be going outside of Magia for the first time."

"Can't you tell us more?" Deanna asked, almost pleading. "We have so much to learn, and Eldrack already knows about all of this."

"Deanna, I have told you before that I can only tell you certain things," Iszarre said sympathetically. "You are learning a lot on your own, and you are becoming very powerful."

Deanna wanted to ask him more questions, but Derek interrupted her. He could tell that Iszarre had told them all that he would, and he wanted to solve the mystery of the ancient voice.

"Now that you're finally awake," Derek said, "we can get going to the library and find out where we need to go."

"Maybe I'm so tired because I stay up studying the Book of Spells," Deanna said quickly. She gathered her things and picked up her backpack. Before Derek could say anything, she got up and headed for the door.

Derek turned toward the door and whispered, "I study, Deanna. You'll find out."

Peekaboo Pepper Books

The line-up of Peekaboo Pepper Books is expanding quickly. We would like to take this opportunity to provide short previews of other upcoming titles in the *Guardians of Elestra* series.

The Dark City: Guardians of Elestra #1

Deanna and Derek follow their grandfather to Elestra where they learn that they are the last hope against a dark wizard in a race to collect the magical moonstones. They'll need all the help they can get from Tobungus, the tap-dancing mushroom man, Iszarre, the powerful wizard/fry cook, and Glabber, the snake wizard. Talking books, book fairies, flying coyote birdmen, devious hot peppers, and a short-tempered frog make their first adventure in Elestra one to remember.

The Desert of the Crescent Dunes: Guardians of Elestra #3 (now available)

Derek and Deanna venture outside of Magia for the first time. They find the Desert Realm to be hot and filled with Eldrack's minions. Their new friend Zorell joins them on the trip, much to Tobungus' dismay. It's a good thing he does, because his dancing proves to be a powerful weapon against Eldrack's army of tentacled sand beasts. Fortunately, the Desert Realm isn't without friends. They meet a resourceful girl named Dahlia who feeds them sugary lizard tails and reads prophecies woven in a hidden tapestry. After finding the entrance to a secret desert, they run into a mysterious statue who points out a solution to their problem. To escape from Eldrack's reach and return the moonstone to the arch, they must cross the Great Snort Pit in a boat scarred with bite marks that are frighteningly large.

The Seven Pillars of Tarook: Guardians of Elestra #4
(available July 2011)

Mount Drasius is cold, very cold, unless you're on the side with the flowing lava. For Derek and Deanna, and their travel partners Tobungus and Zorell, the journey is to the cold side of the mountain. Before leaving Amemnop, they meet the newest member of Glabber's Grub Hut's staff, a pastry chef who seems a little too familiar to the twins. Their quest to find the fourth moonstone starts with a frightening, rubber band-powered ride and includes encounters with jellybirds and rock creatures that are upset by an earthquake that Deanna creates. Once on Mount Drasius, they team up with a band of snowball-throwing kangaroos living near a great temple that just might be the hiding place of the magical jewel they seek. Eldrack's magic looks strong enough to finally defeat the twins, until a pair of sweaty socks powers up Deanna's magic.

The Eye of the Red Dragon: Guardians of Elestra #5 (available July 2011)

The twins and their friends accompany Iszarre to King Barado's castle for a picnic that ends with Iszarre arguing with a peach tree about giving him a second piece of fruit. Their search for the fifth moonstone starts with a trip to Tobungus' home, the Torallian Forest, so Zorell must meditate to find a happy place, and Tobungus needs to feed his shoes flipper juice to increase his dancing abilities. If Tobungus seems weird, his friend Rorrdoogo and the Mushroom wizard Bohootus are stranger yet. But, the real action takes place in the Dragon Realm where a young king finds his way, and his color, and an old dragon gets his mojo back. At the end of their adventure, as usual, Derek and Deanna are left with more questions than answers. Who was this friend who betrayed the older dragon, and where did all of the purple dragon wizards go?

The Misty Peaks of Dentarus: Guardians of Elestra #6
(available August 2011)

A trip to the mountains would be a nice way for
Derek and Deanna to relax after their first five
encounters with Eldrack. Unfortunately, these
are the Antikrom Mountains where time
occasionally goes in reverse, and where valleys
are perfect places for an ambush by Eldrack's
forces. The Iron Forest floats above the highest
peaks, and the twins learn that sometimes the
right jacket is all you need to fly. They meet their
uncle the yak farmer who insists that he must
stay out of the family's battle against Eldrack.
That's too bad because he could tip balance in
their favor.

Author Bio

Thom Jones is the author of the *Guardians of Elestra* series, as well as two forthcoming series, *Galactic Gourmets* (science fiction) and *The Adventures of Boron Jones* (superhero meets chemistry).

He has taught subjects including history, atmospheric science, and criminology at various colleges. What he loves to do most, though, is work with kids. He began writing the *Guardians of Elestra* stories in 2004 for his two sons. The stories evolved, and Tobungus got stranger over the years. He finally decided to start Peekaboo Pepper Books and publish the stories with the view that kids are smart and funny, and that they are more engaged by somewhat challenging vocabulary and mysteries woven throughout the stories they read.

He lives in the Adirondacks with his wife Linda and their three children, Galen, Aidan, and Dinara. He is extremely lucky to have such wonderful editors in Linda, Galen, and Aidan, who have found too many errors to count and have come up with fantastic ideas, even when they don't know it.

51487925R00085

Made in the USA
San Bernardino, CA
23 July 2017